Published by: kindled direct publishing

ISBN: 9798846725690

Library of Congress
Title: Hobbs Lane
Author: Dan Pavao
Registration Date: 2/25/2022
Registration Number: Txu 2-331-470

Other Works by Dan Pavao Include;

Aperture Five

In the Shadow of the Mountain King

Dedicated to my grandchildren. Hoping that you work hard, overcome the challenges in life that everyone must face, and find happiness in family and friends.

Hobbs Lane

(Inspired by the story Quatermass and the Pit, by Nigel Kneale)

by Dan Pavao

Hobbs Lane

Becky lay in her bed and pulled her covers up tightly around her neck. She looked around nervously. Her eyes were drawn instinctively to the dark corners of her room. Corners that never seemed to enjoy the light of the small lamp on her bedside table. Her mother sat next to her and nervously tucked the edges of the eight year old girl's blanket around her small frame. She tried to comfort the girl by her physical presence, but it didn't work, children were more perceptive than that, children could sense the apprehension in their parents and Becky was no exception. Her mother kept tucking anyway.

The room reflected the retro-modern design of the times in which they lived; nineteen sixty six. A green patterned wallpaper adorned the walls which played off the bright yellow coverlet of Becky's bed. Her lamp was a plastic molded teardrop that seemed to hum lightly at her whenever it was turned on.

Becky's mother Linda shifted her gaze from one side of the room to the other with a kind of shaky suspicion. She saw nothing, but kept looking anyway, as if there was something there that couldn't be seen by looking at it directly, but only through the corner of her eye. Every shadow seemed to be a threat that would only manifest if you weren't looking at it. So her head jutted from one corner of the room to the next in a never ending circle. The lamp on the bedside table seemed pitifully inadequate, and Linda wished that she had replaced it a month ago when this had all started. Now, it was too late. The room seemed to threaten the girl and her mother with something oppressive as it surrounded the bed and the light with shadows.

" It's alright. I'll be just up the stairs in case anything happens." said Linda.

" Don't leave me mommy. I don't want to be alone." said Becky.

" We have to try this darling. When I stay down here with you nothing ever happens. We have to know. We have to prove it to your father. Get to bed Becka. I'll be just up the stairs and you can call me any time. If you call I'll be here in just a moment. And I'll have your father close behind." said Linda.

Becky looked disappointed, but she settled down into her bed and looked longingly at her mother as she walked to the door. Her mother smiled at her one last time and she waved to her daughter as she opened the door. Becky waved back lightly and pulled the blankets closer around her neck. She looked around again and crossed herself quickly.

" I'll leave the light on again. Good night darling." said Linda.

The door closed behind her leaving Becky alone in the room. She fought the desire to sleep as long as she could but she was no match for it. Becky drifted off to sleep slowly, and the room remained quiet and peaceful, as if everything that had happened was just a dream. Several hours passed, and Becky's sleep remained undisturbed.

Abruptly, the yellowish light from the incandescent lamp on her nightstand dimmed, seeming to cast a light that was impossibly more yellow. The feeble light of the moon could be seen streaming in from the basement windows high up on the wall. Then suddenly, the bedside lamp dimmed to almost complete darkness, and the room was left in desolate obscurity. It flashed bright again for a moment but then dimmed again, as if the darkness had taken its soul. The clock on her nightstand stopped its ticking. A low rumbling sound permeated the room, seeming to come from everywhere and nowhere. The metal bed posts of Becky's bed creaked and moaned with the movement. Another rumbling of the room came that shook Becky's bed lightly from side to side. Becky struggled awake and sat up in her bed.

" Mom!" screamed Becky.

Suddenly, around the room Becky could see veiled shadowy figures moving on the wall. It was like something cast a shadow on the wall, but there was nothing physically there to cast the shadows, only the shadows themselves. The figures moved in no discernible pattern or blueprint. Just random movements of the impossible shadows on her wall. But most fearful of all was their shape. The figures were roughly humanoid in shape, but had clearly discernible horns protruding from their heads. Moving horned beasts that couldn't be seen were casting the shadows on Becky's wall and in her mind.

The room rumbled again and slowly settled to silence. Then Becky heard the shrieking sounds of the creatures in her ears. High pitched and screeching. Like a sound no human was ever meant to hear. She covered her ears and screamed as loud as she could. Linda and her husband Frank burst open the door and ran into the room. They first looked at their daughter where she sat in her bed, but only a moment passed before they shifted their gaze to the walls of the room. Linda's mouth hung open and Frank's eyes went wide. They could not speak but only stood in place and stared. The shadowed figures against the wall slowly faded to nothingness and the light returned to full brightness. The room appeared normal. It took Linda several moments to recover, then she ran to Becky's bed, grabbed her in her arms and held onto her tightly. Becky hid her eyes against her mother and whimpered lightly in her arms.

" See I told you. You saw it yourself this time." said Linda, turning to her husband.

" I saw it. I wouldn't have believed it. But I saw it."

said Frank, with the slight Irish accent that was a remnant of his childhood.

" This house is cursed. The whole neighborhood is cursed. Everyone says it." said Linda viciously.

" I wouldn't have believed it, but it's true. I saw it with my own eyes. There's nothing left to do then. We've got to move out of here." said Frank.

" Father Garrity said he won't come into the houses in this neighborhood anymore. Margaret Demsel asked him to come and bless her home but he wouldn't come." said Linda.

" There's nothing left to do. We've got to leave. And Becky's sleeping with us until we do. I don't want anyone down in this room anymore. Come on, gather you're things." said Frank.

Linda swept Becky up, blanket and all, and cradled

her.

" Pick up your pillow sweetheart." said Linda.

Linda held her down within reach of the pillow and Becky reached out. Frank held the door open for Linda as she exited the room and climbed the stairs, still holding her daughter. Frank took a last suspicious look around the room. Rage was close to the surface, the rage of a man who would protect his family at any cost, but there was nothing he could do. He closed the door and walked quietly upstairs.

TUNNEL PROJECT

(present day)

The boring machine turned against the dirt wall of the tunnel face beneath Hobbs Lane. It was monotonous and dull to the tunnel workers, an eternal grind that simultaneously induced sleep and gnawed at the nerves. The Hobbs Lane project was a two mile rail extension that would continue the yellow line to a new subway station to be located in the Hobbs district. It was part of a state funded rail modernization project that got the go ahead despite considerable resistance from the neighborhood. It started at the site of the new station and would end, some four months later, when it tied into the existing station down line.

The lighting in the tunnel project always seemed inadequate no matter how many lights were brought in. They cast a dim shadow over the project as workers ran the machinery and monitored the progress of the boring machine. The machine itself was thirty feet in diameter. It cut its way impressively through the earth toward a destination that couldn't be seen but only calculated on paper. Rigging for the boring machine marked the sidewalls of the tunnel and a conveyor moved the earth away from the machine as it inched its way forward on its monotonous journey. Workers busily tended the machine, watched the conveyor, and prepared the metal work for the next length of dirt tunnel that was to be cased with concrete. A dim light could still be seen from the tunnel entrance just a hundred feet back up the tunnel.

Adam walked along the length of the conveyor checking the soil conditions that were expelled by the boring head. It was his job to categorize the soils types they encountered so that they could use the appropriate casing design for the tunnel. It was also his job to watch for out of place materials in the spoils of the boring operation. This included fossil fragments of course which would suspend the project and put them behind schedule. On his last job they had encountered a delay that put them back three months because someone had discovered an old outhouse dating back to the 1800's. A team had come in from the university and literally excavated it, an outhouse! They had been so excited at the prospect, the rational being that everything ended up in the outhouse eventually so it was a great way to discover what the people of the time were doing. As much entertainment as it had given them it had also set them back a month on their schedule, and pushed them into the rainy season. It was unspoken of course, but a fossil fragment was the last thing they wanted to encounter.

As he walked the line of the conveyor he checked the bracing and rigging for the conveyor system. They had

mobilized quickly for the project but the rigging was solid.
The setup crew had done a good job. Suddenly, he saw
something in the dirt passing by on the conveyor and reached
out for it before it passed. He pulled out a bone fragment
about six inches long.

" Holy Christ" said Adam.

He turned to a man standing farther up the conveyor.

" Evilio, you better shut it down." said Adam.
Evilio walked up to where Adam stood looking at the spoils of
the conveyor.

" What's up?" asked Evilio.

" I found a fossil. Last time I was on a project where
we found a fossil they ended up closing the whole thing down
for three months. They got a whole crew in there to excavate
and the whole project got delayed." said Adam.

Adam threw the fossil fragment down to the
tunnel floor.

" Well, just hide it. It's only one bone. Just
pretend that you never saw it. Who's going to know."
said Evilio.

Adam looked up and down the tunnel carefully
and then reached down to the fossil fragment. He picked it
up and put it in his pocket. He gave Evilio a conspiratorial
look and then continued his walk down the length of the
conveyor.

" Damn it." said Adam.

Evilio heard him and stopped, they both looked down to the conveyor and saw a stream of bones and bone fragments passing by. They looked at each other with shared disappointment.

" Shut it down." yelled Evilio.

CIOSED

Three representatives of the Metropolitan transit Authority and the Superintendent of the Bergen Contractors Group stood on the dirt floor of the Hobbs Lane tunnel project. Before them, appearing as a behemoth, was the boring machine in its mechanized splendor. Standing opposite the four was Evan Anderson, Graduate student from Melkin Polytechnic and Principle in charge of the newly formed Hobbs Lane Paleontology Excavation. It was really just graduate students from the University who loved to dig, but you had to name it or the business types wouldn't take you seriously. Evan was aware of that now more than ever. These people could care less about bones in the ground so Evan needed any advantage he could gain.

Richard Daniels, the Superintendent for the Bergen Group, reached out his hand with the keys to access the dig site. He wasn't smiling. What was an incredible find for Evan was little more than an inconvenience for him. Robert Dern from the Transit Authority was also present. He looked on with clear disdain for something that he thought of as little more than a nuisance. A nuisance that he could do nothing to stop.

" Here's the keys. These will get you access to the field office, and the tunnel entrance. Be sure to keep it locked up when no one's here. People will steal anything these days." said Richard.

" I will." said Evan, simply.

" And for God's sake stay away from the boring machine. That's a very expensive piece of equipment. We've got it pulled back away from the tunnel face so you shouldn't have to touch it at all." said Richard Daniels.

" We won't." said Evan.

Evan looked back at the boring machine which had been pulled back 60 feet from the tunnel head and now stood as a megalithic guardian over the dark interior of the tunnel.

" You have 60 days. Don't waste them." said Robert Dern.

" We won't." said Evan

Evan was feeling more uncomfortable by the moment. He prided himself on being accepting of other points of view, but he couldn't help his dislike for these people. They didn't care about anything except schedules and cost overruns. Anything outside of their realm was meaningless to them, which meant that Evan's whole world was inconsequential.

"And see if you can find out why the specimens are located so far down in the ground. We usually don't encounter something like this this far down." said Robert

Dern.

" We'll do our best to give you some answers, but you know the focus of our attention is just getting the specimens out of the ground." said Evan.

Evan was simultaneously excited about the project, anxious about the power of the men standing before him, and bored with their conversation. He wanted their questions to end but he knew that every conversation had to find its own ending.

" You're not allowed to use our tools, you know. We've got the big equipment locked up in a chain link enclosure and the hand tools are locked up inside the field office. Just keep them locked." said Richard Daniels.

" Of course. We have our own gear. There is almost nothing you have that would be useful to us anyway. You have nothing to worry about." said Evan.

" You've got complete control of the site for the next two months and we're going to hold you responsible for anything that's missing or broken when we get it back. Got it?" said Robert Dern.

" I understand." said Evan.

One by one the men gave Evan a skeptical look and then shook his hand and turned away. When the last of them had left Evan breathed a sigh of relief and put the key into his pocket.

Opportunity Knocks

Evan Anderson stood at the front of the boring head and studied the dirt wall. For him this was a dream come true. He needed the field time. For him to find something so close to the University upon which he could base his dissertation was beyond anything he had hoped for. Paleontology was a notoriously hard field to gain recognition in, and major discoveries were few and far between. So what he saw in the earth in front of him was more than just a wall of dirt, it was a glimmer of hope and the chance for recognition that would further his career. His hopes were tempered however, you just never knew what lay beneath the surface, perhaps he would only find more dirt and his time here would be wasted.

Evan studied the dirt wall. He thought he could see a bone fragment just barely visible from the surface. He had a team of sorts. Three undergrad students from the University who had volunteered to be a part of the project. Also, his friend Tom Merril, who also studied Paleontology, had agreed to help with the dig as well. They were using Tom's van for transportation. It was now loaded with equipment that they would need for the dig. The undergrads began unloading the equipment when Tom stepped up next to Evan.

" Do you know what we've got here?" asked Tom

Merril.

"Not really. Only a guess. I've looked at a couple of the specimens. Maybe Australopithecus Africanus. Or Afarensis. We'll know more once we're able to classify them. But right now we've got to get them out of the earth before the subway project starts boring again. They only gave us sixty days and I can probably stall them a little bit after that but eventually they're going to want their tunnel back." said Evan.

"Yea, those guys have no sense of humor. What are they doing so deep in the earth. We must be at least fifty feet down." said Tom.

"Sixty feet. That's the problem. I've sent for Sara Talbert, from the Geology Department. I'm hoping she can give us the answer." said Evan.

"Sara? I know her. Didn't you have a crush on her? Are you sure that's the only reason why you called her?" asked Tom.

"We'll have to set up digging operations down here in front of the boring machine head. And they've given us permission to use the field office on the surface as well. We can catalog and prep there. But everything will be transferred to the University as quickly as possible." said Evan.

"You worked with her on that research project a couple of years ago, didn't you? But she was dating John Philips then. You sure this whole tunnel thing isn't just a reason to get her in a pair of shorts?" asked Tom.

Evan Anderson turned and gave Tom a quizzical look.

" We'll be working long shifts six days a week so make sure that any volunteers are ready to commit to the project. This could be a major find, or it could be nothing at all. Either way they have to agree they're in for the long haul." said Evan.

" You ever see her with her hair down? She always has that ponytail." said Tom.

" Look, she happens to be the best Geologist at the college, if you get away from the tenured professors who never leave campus. She's professional, dedicated, and not the type to skip out to go to a party." said Evan, with some annoyance.

" Right. I'm convinced. You're just ignoring her beauty and only interested in her brains. You ever work on a vertical face like this before?" asked Tom.

" No. Never. But it does have advantages. Fewer backaches." said Evan.

" Yea, even if we find nothing we can write a paper on the techniques of excavation on a vertical surface." said Tom.

" I'd rather find something significant." said Evan.

Evan reached over and pulled out a small scraper from a bucket of tools at his feet. He walked to the tunnel face and began scraping at the earth around the specimen he had been studying. Tom watched him with familiarity and understanding. He knew Evan better than Evan knew himself. Evan was full of ambition and initiative, but under-girding it all was his sense of duty and responsibility. If anyone could excavate the site in two months, it was Evan.

Dirt

The excavation of the tunnel face was in full swing. Two graduate students were involved with the slow process of peeling back the layers of dirt that they hoped would reveal the secrets of ages long gone. It was a snail's pace, but Evan was already pleased with the results. They had uncovered several bone fragments protruding from the tunnel face and were carefully removing the material around them. Tom and another of the graduate students were setting up a process line to catalog, classify, and pack the specimens for shipment. In reality, it was just a makeshift table made from two sawhorses and some wood planking.

Sara Talbert had arrived at the site and agreed to give Evan two days as a personal favor. After that, she would return to her own project. Now as they stood looking at the tunnel face, Evan felt as if he had somehow lost a bet with Tom. She had showed up wearing shorts and with her hair in a ponytail. Tom was right of course. She was beautiful, and Evan suspected that her glasses and studied look of competence were part of a facade. A mask to the beauty that she feared would rob her of the respect and esteem of her colleagues.

" This is where we encountered the first specimens. The boring machine dug them out and the workers were smart enough to realize they needed to call someone. It went to Dean Larson of course, but I'm afraid he's not up to field work anymore. He asked me to give him reports on our progress but otherwise I'm in charge." said Evan.

" Yes. I know Doctor Larson. Don't worry, his name will be all over it in the end." said Sara.

They exchanged a knowing look indicating they'd both seen this happen many times before.

" At this point we've carbon dated some of the material and we're estimating one point three million years. It seems a bit deep though. That's why we called you. We're about 60 feet down and we've never found something like this, this deep. The real question is, was there land movement in this area in the past? Something that would explain the depth we're seeing?" said Evan.

Sara approached the tunnel face and studied it. She pinched off a small handful of the earth and rubbed it between her fingers.

" Could have been. It's really not that unusual. Local subduction. Deposits building on deposits for thousands of years. See this first strata, alluvial deposits. Which

fits in with the geology of the area. You're just lucky you found

it. There are probably a hundred like it in the area that you'll never see." said Sara.

" Makes sense. I guess we'll take our luck and go with it." said Evan.

Blake Thompson, one of the graduate students, was digging at the tunnel face with a scrapper when a large section of earth fell away and hit the ground at his feet.

" Oops. You don't see that happening when you're working flat." said Blake.

The section of earth was approximately two feet long and ten inches across. Blake moved it out of the way carefully, so it could be excavated in turn. Then he noticed the hole that the earth fragment had left. Exposed beneath it was a section of smooth dark blue metallic material.

" What the hell!" said Blake.

He brushed back a bit at the sides to get a better look.

" Evan, come take a look at this." said Blake.

Evan and Sara walked up to the exposed section to study the exposed material. Tom Merril also took notice and joined the two at the tunnel face.

" You ever see anything like that in a dig?" asked Blake.

" No. It must be a pipe or something." said Tom.

" This far down? And in the way of the boring machine. These guys would have mapped out any piping systems in their way. Don't you think?" said Evan.

" Maybe they missed one. Maybe it's so old it doesn't appear on any map." said Tom.

" Doesn't look old. Looks brand new." said Blake.

" That doesn't look like pipe to me. I've never seen a metal like that. At least not on a sewer pipe." said Sara.

" Seen a lot of sewer pipes?" asked Blake.

" Then what is it?" asked Tom.

" I have no idea." said Sara.

Sara moved forward and rubbed her hand on the metal surface, clearing away the earth that had been in contact with the metal for ages. She studied the earth around it carefully. She took Blake's scrapper and used it to expose another four inches of the material, but what she saw and what her experience told her wouldn't come together. There was something curious and out of the ordinary about what they were seeing.

" This is really strange." said Sara.

" What?" asked Evan.

" You said the fossils at this site were over a million years old, correct?" asked Sara.

" Yes. Over a million." said Evan.

" Well this structure, whatever it is, doesn't seem to have disturbed the soil surrounding it. It's homogeneous. It doesn't look like the area was excavated and this structure or pipe put in place. It's like it was already here and the soils deposited naturally around it." said Sara.

" Are you serious? That can't be." said Tom.

Evan moved forward next to Sara. He rubbed the exposed dark blue material with his shirt sleeve.

" Also, this material looks new. It's not corroded at all. If I had to guess I would say it's only been in the ground a couple of years, by the looks of it. It looks like some kind of metal, or alloy. But there's no way a metal is going to be in the ground for even ten years without showing some signs of corrosion." said Sara.

" Maybe another boring? A pipe that was laid sometime in the past that just missed the dig?" suggested

Tom.

" Well, there's one way to find out. Let's excavate it. Try to find the edge of the curve of a pipe. From what we're seeing it looks flat. It doesn't look like a pipe at all. Tom, everyone, we're shifting focus for now. Let's dig around this and expose as much as we can." said Evan.

Night

An old woman stood on the street of Hobbs Lane looking at the temporary modular enclosure of the field office and the fenced off area of the tunnel project. Equipment and materials littered the yard and the tunnel entrance was enclosed by a metal building that would be replaced later with a permanent station. The woman was old but seemed resolute, as if age had never touched her inner resolve. She wore clothing that would have seemed stylish and grand 40 years ago, but now looked thread bare and used. She wore a faded flower pattern hat upon her head that looked like it had been there throughout the course of her life. A faded wool sweater was draped over her form. The woman eyed the area of the tunnel project intently, as if it belonged to her alone and she must protect it. Her face was an expression of hidden knowledge and serious purpose. She was a part of something whose focus was Hobbs Lane, had always been a part of it. Now she stood out the night, never moving, as the moon passed slowly overhead.

Day

Tom Merril had always been the class joker. His mother had told him it was an infantile attempt at avoiding responsibility and he had to agree with her. Still, when he had met Evan in graduate school it was their contrasting personalities that had caused them to become friends. Where Evan was serious, Tom added a sense of mirth. Where Tom was likely to party on the night before a test, Evan would talk him into a semblance of responsibility. Their friendship had been mutually beneficial, even though Tom had the nagging feeling that they would grow apart after they had completed their graduate degrees. So it was fortuitous that Evan had come across this opportunity for the Hobbs Lane dig. They were working on a project now, and it would likely mean they would be friends far beyond their stint at the University. They would collaborate on the research involving Hobbs Lane and both of their names would appear on future research papers.

Tom and the other graduate student's continued to work exposing the blue material exposed in the dig. The uncovered section was now a flat surface ten feet tall and twenty feet wide, but still they had not exposed the edge.

Sara and Evan helped the crew with the excavation. They carried away fossil fragments as they appeared and cleared the way for further excavation. The fossil fragments, once treated like fragile works of art, were now merely piled on the table, as excitement grew with their newest discovery. Sara took photographs every time they exposed another foot of the artifact. The team tried to concentrate on their work but the sight of the material as it was uncovered drew their gaze with growing amazement. The team members glanced at each other periodically. Their conversations became first muted, and then non-existent. The artifact became the elephant in the room. It built from a mere curiosity, to a dominant force that overpowered every thought and emotion. The excitement of the team members seemed to build in the atmosphere to a fever pitch approaching mania. They worked on autopilot. Not really conscious of their efforts until finally, Evan threw down his spade.

" This is crazy." said Evan.

He stopped working and placed his hand against the artifact.

" This isn't a pipe or a culvert. This isn't something that happened to make its way down here in the last decade. This is something else." said Evan.

The cavern was silent as the dig team stopped and weighed the gravity of Evan's statements. They had all been thinking it, but none had dared to speak it aloud.

" Maybe it's a hoax. Something they put here for us to find?" suggested one of the graduate students.

Evan looked at Sara.

" I don't see how someone could implant something like this without massive disturbance of the surrounding soils. You would have to excavate to put it here or plunge it into the ground at high velocity. Either way it's a major disturbance of the soils. There is no differentiation of the soil layers that would explain it." said Sara.

" So if it's not a hoax then what are we looking at?" asked Tom.

" This is no hoax. This is something else." said Evan.

" What are you thinking Evan?" asked Sara.

Silence.

" Just say it." said Sara.

" I can't, not yet. I'm not going to say it out loud yet. But it must have crossed the minds of us all in the last hours." said Evan.

" I've got access to some deep scanning equipment back at the lab. The new software is very accurate. Once we get a reading on how the material reacts, we should be able to get a good picture of its size and shape." said Sara.

" We'll need to call in someone else. Someone who

specializes in something like this." said Tom.

" There's no one who specializes in something like this." said Blake.

" We need John Philips." said Sara.

" Not that guy. He's a jerk." said Tom.

" Yes, but he's also pretty much the smartest guy on the planet. And he's at the University." said Evan.

" And he's still in love with Sara." said Tom.

Sara and Evan both looked over at Tom sharply.

" No he isn't." said Sara.

" Everyone knows it." said Tom.

" Okay. They don't come any better when it comes to physics. And he's good at materials analysis." said Evan.

" You're going to lose it." said Blake.

" What?" said Tom.

" How long do you think you're going to keep this once word leaks out about what we've found. They'll take this away so fast your head's going to spin. And I'm not just talking about the college muckies. The military's going to be in here and take this away in a hot minute. You won't even be able to get in the door." said Blake.

Glances were exchanged throughout the room.

" Ok. We've got to keep this under wraps. No one talks about this outside of our group until we've had a little time to figure out what we have. Once we're sure we have something we'll call a press conference. Or just turn it over to the government. But if we have what I think we have we'll need the best minds in the world working on this." said Evan.

Everyone nodded their heads in agreement.

" I think we need non-disclosure agreements as well. I'll send them out by email tonight." said Sara.

Again everyone nodded in agreement.

As the team went back to work Evan took Tom aside.

" Tom, we can only have people working on this that we trust. We don't fully know what we have yet but I think it's a good idea to pair things back to as few individuals as possible. I know Blake and Jason, but these other two I don't know. Get them to sign the non-disclosure agreements tonight and then tell them we'll ship the fossils to them at the University for analysis. We have to keep the project running in any case so it's no lie. But mostly, I want to get them off of the site." said Evan.

" Okay. I'll take care of it." said Tom.

Watched

Sara and Evan walked out of the tunnel building together. They were exhausted and covered with dirt, but the physical exhaustion was only a minor accessory to the emotional strain they felt. The last ten hours had felt like they had been in a mind blender, turning their thoughts endlessly in a loop that answered none of their questions. Now they felt empty and stressed, with a growing weight that they alone seemed destined to bear. They walked in silence to where their cars were parked inside of the fenced enclosure. Evan searched in his pocket for his keys, but the entire concept of keys just seemed foreign and lost to him. He fumbled and finally pulled them from his pocket.

On the other side of the fence the old woman stood on the street watching them. She seemed a fixture of the street, as if she had been there for her whole existence. She stood waiting for them, and as they approached she began to speak before they even noticed her.

" You don't know what you're doing." said Rebecca Curtis.

Sara and Evan couldn't register any emotion at what should have startled them.

" Who are you?" asked Evan.

" You don't know what you're doing. You're going to ruin it." said Rebecca.

" What are you talking about?" asked Evan.

" Ruin what?" asked Sara.

" Digging about, messing about. I lived there, you know. Right on that site when I was a little girl. I was Becky Simpson then. Now I'm Rebecca Curtis. My family has always lived in this area. We never moved away entirely. I was never sure why, but now I know. I was waiting. Waiting for you." said Rebecca.

" What are you talking about?" asked Sara.

" We're very tired. We'd like to go home." said Evan.

" You found something didn't you? In the hole?" said Rebecca.

Evan started to speak but was interrupted by Sara.

" What do you think we found?" asked Sara.

" It doesn't matter. It's evil what you found. And you better bury it back up before it gets loose." said Rebecca.

The woman turned abruptly and walked away. Sara and Evan watched her walk away slowly in silence.

" What do you suppose she knows?" asked Sara.

" Nothing. What could she know." said Evan.

John Philips

John Philips sat in his University office behind a dark mahogany desk and tapped at his computer keyboard. The desktop was covered from front to back with file folders, stacks of paper, and odd bits of rock and metal samples. John himself almost appeared lost beneath the clutter. He was dressed casually, with reading glass that hung at the edge of his nose. But behind the middle aged exterior was the remnant of an athletic build that could still be seen at the edges and corners. His dark hair graying at the sides gave him the appearance of wisdom, but one look at his eyes denied this immediately. He had that look of a hawk, or a predator, and predators never really looked wise, just hungry. It was perhaps this look that had first attracted Sara to him, that and his stunning intellect, but he was emotionally vacant to the needs of others. As soon as Sara had concluded this, she had left him. They had never resolved why it happened, but Sara knew that John didn't need to have it resolved.

Sara Talbert stepped into the open door and knocked lightly on its surface. She leaned against the door waiting for John's attention. John Philips looked up for only a moment and then shifted his eyes back to his computer screen.

" Hi Sara, how are you?" said John.

" Not bad John, how are you?" said Sara.

" Doing well. Don't be afraid. Come on in." said John.

Sara stepped into the office but remained standing.

" Have you missed me? I knew it was just a matter of time." said John.

" A matter of time before what?" asked Sara.

John Philips shifted his full attention to Sara and removed his reading glasses.

" Before you came running back to me." said John.

" You're so conceited." said Sara, simply.

" I know, but it fuels my intellect so I have to go with it." said John.

" Fuels your ego, you mean." said Sara.

" The girls like it. Hell, I think they expect it. So what am I supposed to do. What's up?" asked John.

" I'm working on a project John, and we need your help." said Sara.

" What's the project?" asked John.

" I can't tell you. But it's big." said Sara.

John focused all of his attention on her.

" What is it?" asked John.

" I've made promises not to discuss it with anyone who's not in the group. So until you agree to help us, and sign a non-disclosure agreement, I can't tell you." said

Sara.

John Philips put his reading glasses back on and
turned to his computer.

" Get someone else. Peter Fry is available I think."
said John.

" We need you." said Sara.

" Well, I'm not going to agree to work with you
without knowing what it is I'm working on." said John.

" I told you. I can't discuss it until you've formally
joined our group." said Sara. " But I guarantee you won't
be disappointed."

John Philips seemed to lose interest and turned
back to his computer screen.

" Just meet me after lunch today and I'll take you
out to the site. Can you find someone to teach your
classes for a while?" asked Sara.

John looked back up at Sara.

" How big is this? And why do you need me?" asked
John.

" We need a physicist. We need someone who's good
at materials analysis. You fit both of those criteria. And you're
close." said Sara.

" Is it government related?" asked John.

" Not yet. So far it's just a private project. University
staff only." said Sara.

" I've got a grad student I can tap but I was going to

use him in the spring. If I use him now I won't be able to use him for an extended vacation I'm planning." said John.

" I guarantee that you won't be disappointed, John. You're going to want to work on this." said Sara with confidence.

" Who else is working on it?" asked John.

" Evan Anderson and Tom Merril. A couple of others." said Sara.

" Paleontology geeks? No way. Those guys are boring. Find someone with lower standards." said John.

" We need you John. Trust me. This is not going to be a waste of your time." said Sara.

Despite his stance, John could sense the importance of the project in Sara's eyes and in her stance. He didn't know anything about it, but he had good instincts for those rare opportunities in life that were few and far between.

" Okay. I'll make you a deal. If I go and I'm not impressed, you have to take a weekend sabbatical with me. Just me and you. For old time sake. If I am impressed, I'll work on the project for as long as it takes." said John.

Sara looked at him with outrage in her eyes. Her right leg shook involuntarily for a moment and she fidgeted with her right hand. He anger was growing exponentially. She shouldn't have been surprised at John's offer, knowing the size of his ego, and she should have walked out of his office, but she also knew that in the end she had the upper hand.

John watched her reaction with a growing sense of alarm. He wasn't sure just how she would react, but he knew that it would tell him something either way. Either she would blow up and leave his office in a fit of exasperation, or they were really dealing with something important.

" Alright. I'll pick you up at one." said Sara, finally.

Sara turned and left the office without another word, but John could sense the anger and determination in the air she had just vacated. He leaned back in his office chair and linked his hands behind his head.

" Wow. They must really have something." said John.

Decision

Evan Anderson opened the lock of the tunnel project exterior enclosure. Sara had brought John Philips to the site with hopes of pulling him into the project. Beyond introductions, they had said nothing about the project to each other. Evan felt it was better just to show him the artifact and let him form his own opinions.

John was becoming more interested in the project by the moment. Not because of anything he had seen or heard, but because of what he had not seen or heard. Most people, he found, would push a narrative they were trying to sell. They would try to hook you or sell you on an idea. You could always tell how important it was in reverse ratio to how hard they sold it. It was his way of reading people and what their intentions really were. Sara and Evan weren't trying to sell the project at all. This meant that whatever they were going to show him was going to sell itself, and this intrigued his intellect, and when his intellect was intrigued his ego took a back seat.

Evan led Sara and John down in the relative darkness of the tunnel. It opened to bright lights, boring gear, and the recent addition of archaeology equipment and tables. Beyond it all was the sheer expanse of the tunnel face looming above them. As they approached, the blue object at the face drew their attention, growing in size as they moved closer. Sara and Evan were still impressed with the immensity of what they had found. They looked at the object with new eyes each time, a renewed sense of shared awe. John Philips looked at the blue surface of the material with a growing sense of apprehension. He exchanged glances with Sara and Evan several times as his mind tried to absorb the reality of what he saw before him.

" How old?" asked John.

" About a million three at the bottom layer of earth. And a million two at the top. The earth isn't disturbed around the artifact. We don't think it was placed here, we think the strata built up around it. We've excavated at top and bottom and as far back as we can to either side. It's eleven feet from top to bottom and we've worked out the size from side to side based on the curvature of the surface. If the curvature remains constant, meaning that it eventually turns out to be a circular structure, then the whole thing is about a hundred and sixty feet across." said Evan.

" Who else knows about this?" asked John.

" So far there are just seven people, all from the University. We know we're going to lose it to the government eventually, but we want to do as much work as we can before we turn it over to them." said Evan.

" We need your help John. We need your background. We need materials analysis." said Sara.

John Philips turned and looked toward Sara. He gave her a sour look.

" Damn it." said John.

Sara only smiled back at him.

" Can you help us?" asked Evan.

John Philips stepped forward and studied the material.

" No sign of pitting or corrosion. It's not a metal." said John.

He reached out with his hand and touched its surface. As his hand made contact with the surface the lights in the tunnel dimmed, as if robbed of power. He removed his hand and the lights returned to normal. He touched it again and the lights dimmed again.

" Did that just happen." said John.

" What?" asked Evan. " The lights? The power is not always steady down here. Not sure why."

" Look at this." said John.

He touched the material again but this time nothing happened. He touched it several more times with no reaction.

" Never mind. Weird." said John.

Evan exchanged a look with Sara.

" Can you help us?" asked Evan.

" When do we start?" asked John.

" Right now. We're pressed for time as it is." said

Evan.

Examination

Sara and Blake were busy setting up equipment for the deep geologic scan. An array of sensors and actuators screwed into the dirt wall of the tunnel face, all tied back to a terminal and display system set up at a table. John Philips spent his time with his own testing equipment at the blue metallic substance they had uncovered. Applying varying chemicals and testing for conductance and magnetic properties. He had been like a man possessed since he signed on to the project. In some sense, John had waited his entire life for this question, now it was here before him and it consumed every thought in his mind. It showed in his eyes, and his face, and in his demeanor. Everyone and everything around him was just another tool to find the answers to the questions staring him in the face.

" Is this ground penetrating radar?" asked Evan.

" Yes. Partially, but the software is what really makes this system unique. It's new and far more advanced. The software can distinguish the different refraction patterns of known materials. It pings again and again and the software builds an image from the pulses and refraction patterns. It keeps building and building until we get a picture of the surrounding strata. All in a matter of seconds. We end up with a three dimensional image that can wrap around an object. In this case our uninvited visitor here. We're still working on it but it's almost ready for prime time." said Sara.

" Wow. How come we've never heard of this?" asked Evan.

" You're in paleontology." said Sara.

" Of course." said Evan.

" If they think they can find oil with it, they'll fund it." said Sara.

" So you think we'll get a three dimensional image out of this?" asked Evan.

" We should. And we're about ready." said Sara.

Sara finished checking the last connections on the back of her equipment.

" Dr. Philips. Dr. Philips. Can you stand away from the artifact for a moment." said Sara.

" Sure." said John.

John stepped back from the blue face of the artifact and watched while Sara set and calibrated her equipment. Everyone stopped what they're doing and looked expectantly at the tunnel face. Sara pushed a button on the equipment and there was a momentary click that seemed to vibrate through the whole tunnel. The lights dimmed briefly, then flickered a moment before coming back on. The cables leading to the actuators and sensors jumped as if stressed by some unseen force.

" Did your equipment cause that?" asked John.

" I've never seen that happen before. It shouldn't
have. We're not pulling that much juice to begin with." said
Sara.

A moment of silence followed in which everyone
in the tunnel exchanged glances. They felt a part of
something that was beyond comprehension.

" Did you get what you needed?" asked John.

" Yes. It'll take a couple of minutes for the
software
to build the picture." said Sara.

" Well, in the meantime I can tell you what you don't
have here." said John.

" What do you mean?" asked Evan.

" From a materials perspective. It means that I don't
know what it is but I do know what it isn't. You don't have a
metallic material. It's not electrically or magnetically
conductive. My best guess is that it's some type of ceramic
blend. But whatever it is, it's very tough. Resistant to acids and
bases. Resistant to heat and cold. And with a physical
structure that is as hard as diamond. I'll need some special
equipment to get an actual sample of it. Look here where I've
tried to scratch the surface." said John.

John Philips stepped forward and pointed to the
surface of the dark blue material.

" I gave this several good whacks with a hammer and

chisel and couldn't even scratch it. Even the hardest of materials would have shown a scratch." said John.

" Pictures coming through." said Sara.

Everyone moved back to the monitoring equipment and lined up behind Sara. Jason remained behind looking at the blue material where John had pointed just moments before.

" We're getting a good picture here. Took the computer a couple of minutes to figure it out but now it's coming through." said Sara.

On the screen they could see a three dimensional image taking shape. A round disk shape, flat on top and bottom with no other appendages or external features.

" How accurate is this?" asked Tom.

" It should be pretty accurate. It looks like what we're seeing exposed is pretty much what we're going to see around the entire structure." said Sara.

" It's not very aerodynamic. No taper at the leading edges. John, do you think something like that could have flown?" asked Sara.

" Not by conventional means. But then we don't know anything about it yet. It's an artifact. Assuming it has an extraterrestrial origin, it could have been built on the site." said John.

" A base? An outpost?" asked Sara.

" No telling. But if we're going to learn anything at all

about it, we've got to get inside. We have to explore the interior." said John.

" We need to find an opening. There has to be one. Right. Something had to get inside, or outside." said Evan.

" Tunnel around it?" said Tom.

" Hey guys!" said Jason.

" That's a lot of excavation. It's going to go well beyond the perimeter of the tunnel project. Also, we aren't going to have that kind of time." said Evan.

" What if the openings on the top?" asked Tom.

" Hey guys, you should come and look at this." said Jason.

They all turned and looked at Jason where he stood next to the artifact.

" There's something here. An outline of something in the surface." said Jason.

The small group rushed to where Jason stood looking at the face of the artifact. They began to trace the outline. It was rectangular in shape, approximately five feet by two feet, and oriented like a doorway.

" This is where John was testing. Was it here before?" asked Evan.

" No. I'd have seen this. And I've been studying this thing for hours." said John.

" It's in the shape of an opening. It's definitely door shaped." said Tom.

"How could it just show up that way?" asked Sara.

"What are the chances we would happen to excavate right at the door location anyway?" asked Tom.

"I'm telling you it wasn't here before." said John.

"Look there's a smaller door in the center." said Sara.

The group focused on the outline of a small box shape in the center of the larger outline. It was a square approximately ten inches to a side.

"Get me a spatula." said Evan.

Jason grabbed a flat spatula from the survey table and handed it to Evan. Evan began to probe at the smaller outline. He pried at its edges, trying to open it like a panel cover. After several minutes of trying he stopped and stepped back.

"We might try something heavier, but I couldn't get it to move at all." said Evan.

At that moment the panel opened along the edges of the smaller outline and slid out like a drawer. Everyone jumped back, Evan almost knocking Tom down. John Philips moved forward carefully to look into the open drawer. He peered inside a moment, and then reached in his hand.

"Careful." said Tom.

"John, don't." said Sara.

John pulled something out of the inner recess of the

drawer. It was small, oval and roughly shaped. John studied it for several moments.

" What is it?" asked Sara.

John turned it over several times in his hand.

" It looks like . . . It looks like a biscuit." said John.

" A what?" asked Evan.

" It looks like a biscuit. Ancient and petrified. It's as hard as a rock. But it looks like a biscuit." said John.

Sara reached forward and took the object from John's hand.

" It does resemble a biscuit." said Sara.

" Are you saying we uncovered an ancient extraterrestrial bakery?" asked Tom.

The earth began to shake and rumble around them. The small group scrambled on their feet to remain standing. The lights in the tunnel dimmed and flickered erratically. The larger outline on the artifact became a door that slid inward and then moved to the side, revealing the interior within. The interior of the artifact was pure white, contrasting sharply with the dark blue of the exterior. The white interior was so intense that it seemed to glow with a light of its own. The group didn't move for several moments as they tried to assess the new situation. They simply looked on with stunned faces. John Philips was the first to recover. He moved forward slowly, an inch at a time, to try and peer inside the artifact.

" Maybe we better think about this." said Tom.

" What's the matter? Haven't you ever wanted to see the inside of a bakery before." said John.

Evan recovered next and began to follow John into the artifact.

" Just be careful John." said Evan.

John looked at him sharply, and then continued to inch his way through the door opening.

Sara recovered next and began to follow Evan. John moved into the interior first and moved his head around to take in the scene. The interior space was square shaped with approximately fifteen feet to each side. The ceiling was low by human standards at approximately six and a half feet. The corners of the room and transitions between floor and ceiling were rounded, giving the area a gentle comforting feel. The space was illuminated by a soft glow that seemed to be everywhere, but there was no apparent source for the light. As the group progressed into the room they could see the desiccated and shriveled remains of two human bodies in a corner. The bodies were shriveled almost beyond recognition, with stringy hair in mats over the head and parts of the body. With the exception of the desiccated bodies, the room appeared empty. John took another step into the room followed by the others.

" Are they human?" asked John.

Evan stepped forward to take a closer look at the

remains.

" Yes. Africanus by the look of them. Of course we've never seen one in this good a shape before." said Evan.

" This good a shape?" said Sara.

John Philips looked around at their surroundings.

" How did they get here?" asked John.

" Well there's no doubt anymore on what we've found, is there? Even if we believed that this thing was placed here in modern times, there's nothing that would account for finding the remains of two prehumans inside of it. This thing must be at least as old as the bodies." said Sara.

" And look at the technology we're seeing. Look at the way the door is attached to the wall. I've never seen a hinge like that." said Tom.

They all turned to take a closer look at the door where it was in contact with the wall. It was attached at the top and bottom but the door seemed to just meld together with the wall at these points. As if the door and wall surface were part of the same piece.

" There's no hinge or moving parts that I can see. It's like an organic connection, the door moving aside as a part of the wall." said Tom.

" And look at where the drawer opened. The drawer came out at least ten inches and retracted back into the door when it opened. But the door is only about five inches thick?"

said Sara.

"Does anyone see a light source in here? The space is well lit, but I can't figure out where the light source is coming from?" said Evan.

"You think it's emanating from the wall?" asked Sara.

"I don't know. But I know we don't have the technologies we're seeing here." said Evan.

For the first time, fear crept into the group and replaced the prevailing feeling of fascination that they shared. None of them were prepared for what they were seeing. There was no training for extraordinary experiences, no background to rely on, no shared knowledge that would prepare them for what they were seeing. Their small group was taking on the most monumental discovery in the history of the planet, and they were doing it alone.

Field Office

The group gathered in silence in the field office. The mood in the room was one of disbelief and bewilderment. Their faith in a world view they had lived with their entire lives was crushed within seconds. Tom sat at the central table and was lost in his own thoughts. Sara and Evan leaned against the row of file cabinets along one wall. Neither of them knew what to say. John Philips paced the floor slowly. Usually full of confidence and direction, John was lost in his own inability to understand what they were seeing. Blake entered the office with bags of food and put them on the table, but no one moved toward them.

" I know what we're all thinking, but no one wants to be the first to say it." said Sara.

She gave Evan a questioning look. No word passed between them but Evan understood that she expected him to take the lead for the group.

" Yea." said Evan, reluctantly. " For the record, this thing is of alien origin."

" So what's it doing here? Buried in the earth for a million years. Why was it put here? What were they trying to do?" asked John.

" An even bigger question is why is it still active after all this time? Why did it suddenly just turn itself on? What power supply is it using that would still be active after a million years?" said Sara.

" I've got a theory about your last question. We've all noticed the brownouts in the lighting that seem to happen around this thing. I saw in the paper yesterday that the brown outs have been happening city wide, not just down in the tunnel. I think it's somehow able to steal power from whatever power systems it finds around it. Some kind of wireless energy transfer." said John.

" You think that it's been keeping itself alive by stealing power from the power systems around it? For a million years?" asked Sara.

" I don't know what it's been doing for a million years, but I think it's been stealing power now. Absorbing it from the power grid." said John.

" My question is why was it trying to capture primitive humans in the first place?" asked Evan.

" What do you mean?" asked Sara.

" Well. When we first opened the small door and the drawer popped out, John found what looked like a biscuit inside. And when the larger door opened we found two primitive humans inside. I think that whatever it was doing a million years ago involved luring and capturing primitive humans." said Evan.

" What were they doing with them?" asked Sara.

" I don't know." said Evan.

" Do you think it's time we turned this over to the government?" asked Tom.

The question hung in the air. Tom looked up and met the gaze of everyone in the room one by one. Everyone knew what they should do, but the energy in the room was going in the opposite direction.

" If we do, we'll never see this site again. This thing will go classified in a hot minute." said John.

" It's just a matter of time." said Blake.

" Not now. We've got the expertise for this. We can work this project a little longer." said John.

" I think we should take a vote." said Evan.

Evan looked around the room and met with no opposition.

" All those in favor of turning this thing over to the government now, raise your hands." said Evan.

Tom Merril raised his hand. The others did not.

" Ok. We'll keep it in the family for a little bit longer. But we have to have a game plan. We need the resources of the University to do any serious analysis on the bodies we found. And the minute we haul these into the lab, it's over. Word will spread like wildfire." said Evan.

" I've got some lab equipment here. We can do some simple testing and have a look through a microscope. But all my heavy equipment is back at the University." said Sara.

" Okay. Detailed analysis is going to take more time anyway, but we'll do what we can. More than anything else, we need to stabilize them. Prevent any further degradation. Tom, can you oversee this?" asked Evan.

" Sure." said Tom.

" I'm still involved with materials analysis. Tom is going to help me, and Blake is going to keep excavating around the structure. No one new is to be added to the project. You got that?" said Evan. " We're going to have a hard enough time keeping this quiet for a couple of weeks."

" And I'm going home. I'm exhausted." said Sara.

Evan looked at his watch.

"It's past ten. Sara is right. Let's work until eleven and then figure on meeting back here tomorrow at six." said Evan.

" That's not even eight hours from now!" said Blake.

" We've only got this dig site for a limited amount of time, and it's even less if this leaks out to anyone. We've got to take advantage of every minute we have." said Evan.

" He's right." said John.

" Blake and I are staying to get a material sample of the white interior. I want to drop it off at the University tomorrow. Blake, it won't take long then you can go home and get some sleep." said Tom.

" Okay. We're all tired and stressed, but we're under a time crunch. And we have no idea how long this secret is going to last." said Evan.

Evan looked around the room. He could see the exhaustion and fatigue in each of them. He knew they couldn't go on this way for much longer. Something would give. Exhausted minds make stupid mistakes, and they had no room for error.

Past

Evan and Sarah walked across the packed earth that served as the parking lot of the Hobbs Lane tunnel project. They moved in the slow and painful steps of the truly exhausted. They didn't discuss it, but in both their minds was the memory of the old woman who had met them the day before. Though they had tried to dismiss her as just some crazy person, but her words still reverberated in their minds. In some way she seemed to be a part of the whole mystery of the artifact. She was intertwined with its story, and it was personal for her. She had significance that they could not measure.

Evan unlocked the chain link gate that secured the facility, walked back inside the enclosure and entered his car to move it out of the compound. Sara followed in her own vehicle. Evan stopped his car to re-close and lock the gate when he saw someone on the street ahead of them. The old woman stood at the edge of the shadows. Sara exited her car and stood next to Evan.

" Is that her?" asked Sara.

Rebecca Curtis moved out of the shadows and began to speak.

" You haven't stopped digging have you?" said Rebecca.

" Who are you?" asked Evan.

" We've talked before. I told you to stop. But you don't know what you're doing." said Rebecca Curtis.

" What do you want?" asked Evan.

" I want it to stop." said Rebecca Curtis.

" What do you think we're doing?" asked Sara.

" You're digging, aren't you? But you don't know what you're digging up do you? I may not have the smarts that you have. I may not have gone to a fancy college. But I know things that you don't. And I know when to listen to the warnings that the body gives. You should stop what you're doing before you find something you don't want to find. Before you cause damage that you can't undo." said Rebecca.

" What do you know about what we dug up?" asked Sara.

" You ask stupid questions. I know what you're doing. I've always known this was coming. I told you, that's why I stayed around this place . . . waiting for it. You're digging in the earth in an area where no one should be digging. I'm telling you, I've lived around here all my whole life and I've seen it. There's evil down there. Nothing good. And it doesn't matter what you do with it. It's evil and it's all going to turn out bad. Do you hear me? Bad! You have to stop now. Before it goes any further. You have to stop." said the old woman.

" What do you know about all this?" asked Sara.

" I told you. I've lived here since I was a little girl. I've seen things. The whole neighborhood saw them. Demons. There are demons in the depths. Look around you. Why do you suppose this area has always been poor? No one lives around here, or very few. No one wants to live around here, do you get it? Everyone who buys around this place thinks they're getting a good deal. But they always sell their properties within a couple of months. And usually for less than they paid. Don't you see? It's the demons they see. You mark my words, and stop what you're doing in the earth." said Rebecca Curtis.

" We're not doing anything. We're scientists. Whatever's there in the earth was there long before we came." said Evan.

" You don't deny it now do you? Come with me. I want to show you something." said Rebecca Curtis.

The old woman turned and began walking down the street. Sara and Evan hesitated. Rebecca Curtis stopped and turned to look at them.

" Come on. It's a short trip. I won't bite you." said the old woman.

Sara and Evan looked at each other for a moment and then without a word between them they followed behind her.

Rebecca Curtis walked with the sureness of someone who not only knew the street, but was a part of its life and breath. A screeching stray cat was ignored. She feared no shadow and no sound. The abandoned cars that sat rotting in their place were merely a part of the life she led. They neither offended or outraged her. They were like familiar friends she had grown old with.

She led them down the street to an old broken out house. Shabby and gray, neglected and uninhabited for years.

" This used to be my house at one time. A long time ago. Now I live two blocks over. Better area, but not by much. Come." said Rebecca Curtis.

She led them through the broken front door, stepping carefully over debris and detritus that littered the floors. The interior appeared to have been ransacked long ago. Junk and trash littered the dwelling with the remnants of broken furniture strewn about randomly. Wallpaper was visible, but only as remnants peeling from the walls. Rebecca picked up a small electric lantern from the floor.

" I put this here before. I was planning on this meeting." said the old woman.

She turned on the small portable lantern and led them down a stair that creaked so loud with her footsteps that Evan and Sara hesitated to follow her. After a moment's hesitation, in which the stair didn't collapse, they followed to a basement room at the bottom. The room was empty except for the remains of an old nightstand that had broken up long ago.

" This was my room once. It's seen better days. Look at the drawing on that wall." said Rebecca Curtis.

Sara and Evan looked at the wall and saw dark drawn images of horned beasts. Shadow like creatures, outlines of something unseen in the night. An adumbration of something feared and whispered about.

" This is what you'll find down there. If you keep digging. This is what you'll face. There are drawings like this in other basements around here as well. I've seen them. My neighbor down the street had her granddaughter living in a basement room. One night they heard sounds of something moving. Bumping grinding sounds. Then the earth starts to move. They run for the little girl but they're too late. They find the girl in the closet crying and whimpering about the demons. Poor little thing had pulled out her own hair." said Rebecca.

Sara and Evan listen with interest.

" Yes. She had just sat in that closet pulling out all her hair while the demons howled around her. Little girl's scalp was bloodied and raw when they took her to the hospital." said Rebecca.

" What happened to you?" asked Sara.

" We lived here once. Like I said. But my parents moved to a new house a couple of streets down." said Rebecca.

" This is crazy. Just urban legends. Horned beasts? This is just someone's imagination running wild." said Evan.

" No. I've seen it. It was real." said Rebecca.

Evan and Sara exchanged a look of concern. If only they felt as confident in their assertions as the old woman felt in hers.

" You can go now if you want. But take my advice and stop digging. Just bury up whatever you've found and leave it alone." said Rebecca.

Sara and Evan stood silently for several moments trying to process what they had just heard. As if to fill the void, Sara muttered, " Thank you." quietly. The old woman shrugged and walked out of the house without saying another word. Evan and Sara stirred back to life and made their way out onto the street. They walked back to where their cars were parked.

" Crazy old woman." said Evan.

" Do you think she is Evan? You know what we've dug up down there. And John thinks it's able to absorb power from the surrounding environment. What if it was having an impact on this neighborhood? What if she's telling the truth? What if it's been the cause of problems in this neighborhood for years?" said Sara.

" It's just fear and superstition. An irrational reaction to the unknown. Urban ghost stories." said Evan.

" Evan, maybe we should turn it over to the

government? Just remove ourselves from this altogether." said Sara.

" Do you think they would bury it up?" asked Evan.

" Then maybe we should bury it." said Sara.

" You think the transit authority will just drop a million dollar project? They were about to hit it with the boring machine. We can't bury it." said Evan.

" Then we should just walk away from this. I have a bad feeling about the whole thing." said Sara.

" Okay. First demon we see. We'll walk away. You have my word on it." said Evan.

Grinder

Blake walked into the interior of the alien device carrying a small hand held grinder. He was feeling less confident with each passing moment he spent inside the artifact. Paleontology was supposed to be boring and monotonous work! Fossils weren't supposed to cause blackouts or be related to alien technology. It wasn't what he signed up for, but now he was caught in the moment and the momentum of the group. Despite his fear, he couldn't back out now. They were volved in something that would be a milestone of history for a thousand years.

Blake pulled and tugged on an electrical cord behind him. He looked around briefly, and then set his small canister against the sidewall to catch the grindings from the white wall material he would be grinding. He brought the grinder up and switched it on. He brought it up to the wall surface and worked it up and down the wall. Then he checked the small container for grinding material. The container was empty so he began grinding again. Suddenly, he felt a vibration that seemed to shake through the walls and floor of the structure. He stopped grinding and looked around, unsure of what he had actually felt. The shaking subsided. Blake considered for a moment, but then slowly brought the grinder up against the wall. He cautiously started grinding again and the shaking and vibration returned. Blake stopped immediately and the vibration slowly receded to nothing. Now Blake knew that something significant was taking place. It wasn't just his imagination or the movement of the grinder. The whole room or structure itself seemed to be shaking. A part of his mind knew that he should stop, he should wait for the others to document what was happening, but another part of his mind couldn't resist the temptation and allure of seeing what would happen if he tried it just one more time. He brought the grinder up against the wall and carefully started grinding. The shaking started again. Stronger this time. The shaking and vibration built in intensity until the entire structure was shaking. Blake steadied himself against the side wall and tried to ride it out. He struggled to maintain his balance. A deep rhythmical sound started, like a background noise to the vibration. Blake wasn't sure if the sound was real or only in his head. Suddenly, the electrical cord lifted off of the floor and the grinder was pulled from Blake's hands. It dangled at high speed in the air just inches from his face. The floor seemed to move and bounce under him. Blake was hit with a sharp pain in his head causing him to grab at his temples. His muscles tightened in pain. He slid slowly down the wall of the room until he lay on the floor. Suddenly, he was not in the alien artifact any longer, he wasn't in the tunnel project, and he wasn't himself.

Blake looked around the kitchen of his old home when he was ten years old. He sat at the dinner table across from his mother who served him another piece of chicken onto his plate. At first he looked around the room, looked at his hands, and tried to piece together what had happened. The ten year old Blake wondered what was happening, but only for a moment, as the reality of his circumstances was beyond question, his other life a mere dream. He looked at the familiar face of his mother sitting across from him. She had died long ago, but he couldn't deny what his eyes were seeing. His mother smiled at him and went back to her meal. Blake smiled in turn and forgot about his other life. He became the ten year old child again sitting at the dinner table with his mother. He reached for his fork and began to dig into his food. He looked at his mother again and saw her staring at him.

" You took the last piece of chicken." said Blake's mother.

" No I didn't, you gave it to me." said Blake.

His mother smiled at him, and then something happened. Something changed in the air around them. Around the kitchen walls he saw the shadowed images of demons. Shadows of horned beasts that menaced the very atmosphere of the room. He looked back to his mother with growing fear. Her smile seemed to get bigger and bigger on her face. Finally, her smile stretched impossibly from ear to ear. She opened her mouth and revealed sharp teeth in the long row of her smile. Human teeth that looked like they had been filed to a sharp point.

" I'm still hungry." said Blake's mother.

The ten year old Blake looked in silence at his mother's hungry stare. He shivered with fear, like prey trembling before a predator. Suddenly she lunged across the table at him.

Inside the Device

Tom Merrill shook Blake lightly, trying to wake him.

" Blake!" said Tom, loudly.

Blake's body seemed lifeless. Tom felt at his neck for a heart beat and was relieved to feel his pulse beating strongly. He shook Blake again.

" Hey, Blake!" said Tom.

Blake opened his eyes slowly and saw Tom kneeling before him. Tom smiled. Relieved that his friend was responding. Blake's body shuddered from head to toe. He tried to speak but no words would come from his mouth.

" What happened?" asked Tom.

Blake shook and shivered at the power of his dream. He struggled to get up but Tom held him down. Blake shook uncontrollably, and his eyes darted wildly from side to side.

" Are you alright?" asked Tom.

It seemed that Blake was struggling to talk, but no words would form in his mind. Tom steadied Blake by the arms and dragged him to his feet. He nearly carried him out of the artifact. After several yards Blake began to carry more of his own body weight and the two made it to the field office before stopping to rest. Tom sat Blake down in a chair and sat next to him to catch his breath.

" I'm going to get the others." said Tom, and he left the room not waiting for a reply.

Within minutes the group was in the field office sitting around Blake who looked visibly shaken. He looked haggard and emotionally exhausted, but he was beginning to calm down and the shaking they had observed in him was less. He sipped at a water bottle and starred at hands as if he was a million miles away.

" You saw the grinder just lift into the air?" asked John.

" Yes. It was floating in the air in front of me. It came out of my hands. I thought it was going to grind into my face." said Blake. He gestured in front of him with his hands, as if holding a drill.

" It moved on its own. I'm telling you that thing is intelligent. When I started to use the grinder the whole room shook. That thing attacked me. It got into my head." said Blake, who was visibly flustered. His head moved in jerking cadence with his words.

" And you think all this happened in response to your grinding on the interior wall surface?" asked John.

" I can't know that that was what caused it. It moved. The whole room moved, like it was alive! The grinder came off the floor all by itself. Then it was in my head. It was like I was ten years old again. A dream . . . a nightmare. I saw my mother. I saw images, small horned beasts. Standing upright. Demons. They were surrounding us. Then she became a demon too." said Blake.

Blake lowered his head to the table and sobbed. He covered his face with his hands and cried quietly.

" You're okay now, Blake. It's all over." said Sara.

Sara put her hand on Blake's back and rubbed him gently. She looked at Evan with concern in her eyes.

" Let's send Blake home to get some rest." said Evan.

Tom Merril stirred for the first time.

" I'll drive him home." said Tom.

Tom helped Blake get up from his chair and helped steady him with his arm around his shoulder. He looked briefly at Evan and Sara. It was a look they shared more and more as the days progressed. It was a look of seriousness, and weight, and gravitas. It was a look that said they were in way over their heads.

" Get some rest Blake." said Sara.

The others watched quietly as Tom and Blake left the room. When they were gone the conversation began again.

" You realize we're talking about telekinesis and telepathy here. Something with enough psychic power to lift a grinder off the floor?" said Sara.

" But what's the source? Are we talking about

telekinesis from the artifact itself? A million year old artifact? How could it do that?” asked Evan.

“ I don't know, but it's pretty obvious that it couldn't have come from any other source. I don't know what we have here, but I think we're in over our heads.” said Sara.

“ We were in over our heads several days ago. Everyone is over their heads with this. This is totally new and unheard of.” said John.

“ Like the artifact was alive. Isn't that what Blake said?” said Sara.

“ We're getting ahead of ourselves. We don't really know what happened in there.” said Evan.

“ How could the device act that way? How could it use telekinesis? How could it push Blake into a dream?” asked Sara.

“ We have more questions than answers right now. We can't be emotional about this. We have to stay rational and analyze it like any other problem in science.” said Evan.

“ Demons! That's what Blake said, isn't it? Demons. Anyone have any comment on that?” asked Sara, loudly.

“ Fear induced psychosis. You heard him talk about his dream! What do you think it was? He got frightened, he's exhausted, he fell down and lost consciousness, and his imagination took over from there. He probably didn't even see the grinder lift off of the floor. Why look for something complicated and supernatural when the simplest solution is usually the right one? You know of Holcomb's razor?" said John.

Sara looked at Evan, as if prompting him to respond.

" We talked to a woman in the street the other day. She appears to have lived in this area her entire life. She told us a story similar to what Blake reported. Demons. People seeing dark shapes and horned beasts in the shadows. Monsters in their basements." said Evan.

" Is that fear induced psychosis as well? She begged us to stop digging. She said that we would release the demons." said Sara.

" Well, we can give her that one. We're not digging anymore." said John.

" Yes, but it doesn't hide the fact that she knows something about what's going on here. That the story Blake told us has remarkable similarities to the stories she told." said Sara.

" What is it you think she knows besides legends and stories? She doesn't know anything. There have always been myths and legends. And in the end they're usually easily explained by science." said John.

" Those legends and stories came from somewhere. That's what she knows." said Sara.

Sara and John squared off at each other.

" Okay. Let's look at this logically for a minute. Let's break it down to a scientific problem. Now, what do we know for certain about the device?" asked Evan.

" We don't know anything for certain. We know that we have a device. We're pretty sure it's of extraterrestrial origin, but we don't know that for sure. It may be a space ship, but we don't know. We don't know what it's made of, but we're pretty sure it's not metallic. We don't know how it got here and we don't know what it was doing here to begin with." said John.

" But we do know a couple of things. We know that it was interested in early human life on our planet. We know that it came here for a reason, though we can only guess at what that reason might be. We know that it is still active after a million plus years of sitting unused in the earth. And I think it's safe to assume that it's the cause of the power outages we've been seeing throughout the city." said Evan.

" We've detected no increased levels of radiation in the area. It's drawing power off the grid in some way that is unfamiliar to us." said Sara.

" I think we can also assume that it can use the power it's been pulling in ways that we would consider impossible. Psychic potential, telekinesis, whatever you want to call it." said Evan.

" Could it have been pulling power off the grid all these years? Maybe keeping itself active. Waiting. Could the rumors and legends of this area be true? It seems like it's too much of a coincidence for it not to be." said Sara.

" There's something else." said John.

" What?" asked Sara.

" I think that whatever purpose it had when it lured in the cave men… " said John.

" Africanus." interjected Evan.

" Africanus. I think it's still running the same program." said John.

" You mean that whatever purpose it had back then, it has the same purpose now?" asked Sara.

" Exactly. If it's still active after all this time then it would make sense that it's still following its original design." said John.

" I agree. So what we really need to figure out is, why was it sent here? And what is its purpose?" asked Evan.

" I think we need to turn this over to the authorities." said Sara.

" No. I keep telling you. There are no experts for something like this. We're the experts. And we're probably going to be a lot more careful than anyone the government would pull in." said John.

" Yea. But if someone's going to blow this place up in the process of studying it I'd sure rather it be them and not us." said Sara.

" Should we vote again?" asked Evan.

" Tom's not here." said Sara.

" Let's see how the vote comes out without him. All those in favor of turning this over to the authorities raise your hand." said Evan.

Sara raised her hand and then stared in desperation at the other two.

" It's not a fair vote without Tom." said Sara.

" Then we'll wait for Tom." said Evan.

" We should be talking about next steps. Provided that we vote to continue our research." said John.

" What next step do you want to take?" asked Sara.

" Well, we're inside the device, but obviously there's a lot more that we're not seeing. We have to find a way to open it. Find out what's behind the room that opened up." said John.

" What's your suggestion?" asked Evan. " We just sent Blake home because he used a grinder on the wall. We can't just start drilling or hammering on the thing. God knows what would happen."

At that moment Tom Merril opened the field office door and ran into the room, struggling to regain his breath.

" Something's changed. You better come look." said Tom.

Tom turned without waiting and ran out the door. The others hesitated only a moment before following. Tom led them down the stair and past the boring machine and into the all white room of the artifact. Inside the room, opposite the main entrance there was now a circular plate on the wall. The circle was approximately 12 inches in diameter with a dark background. Inside the circle were ten smaller circles lining the perimeter. Each was multicolored with ten separate colors like pie slices emanating out from the center. A larger multicolored, circle occupied the center.

" When did this get here?" asked John.

" I have no idea. I walked Blake to his car and he felt a bit better, so I let him drive home. Then I came down here to check the wall where Blake had been grinding. And there it was." said Tom.

" What is it?" asked Sara.

" And how did it just appear?" asked Evan.

Evan walked up to the new feature on the wall and studied it. John followed him. Evan reached out and turned one of the circular plates. It spun easily.

" I think it's a puzzle." said John.

" A puzzle?" asked Evan.

" A puzzle. Or a sophisticated cipher lock. Look, if you spin each of the circles on the outside, a different color comes into contact with the central circle. Then if you spin the center circle you can make all of the colors line up with the
colors on the outer circles." said John.

" What happens then?" asked Sara.

" Who knows. But there's only one way to find out." said John.

John sat on the floor and began to spin the outer circles, trying different combinations and then trying to align the central circle.

" Maybe this isn't such a good idea." said Tom.

" This could take some time." said John.

" Maybe this isn't something we should be playing with." said Sara.

" Where's your sense of adventure Sara. What's the worst that could happen." said John.

" Just ask Blake." said Sara.

" John, maybe she's right. Maybe we should leave it alone for now." said Evan.

" Relax. This is what science is all about." said John.

They watched in silence for a moment. Each with their own thoughts and feelings about the wisdom of moving forward with the device. In their minds they knew they couldn't predict the outcome of their actions, or the chain of events that may happen as a result, but there was something inside that pushed them just one more step farther before they would stop, before they would all agree they had gone too far.

" This should do it." said John.

John finished spinning the last of the outer circles and then moved the inner circle into alignment. The colored segments of the outer circles now matched up with the colored segments of the inner circle. Suddenly, they heard a noise like the popping of breakers from outside the device. Evan looked through the open doorway.

" We lost power to the main building." said John.

" Probably to the whole city this time." said Sara.

The interior walls of the device still glowed with a soft white light. The circular object on the wall abruptly melded into the seamless wall surface. John Philips jumped to a standing position. A seam appeared in the wall before him and a doorway opened as the seam seemed to absorb into the wall surface. A new room was now visible through the new opening created in the wall. John was the first to recover his composure. He took a tentative step to the opening and carefully peered inside.

" Oh my God." said John.

John Philips stepped fully into the room. Evan looked at Sara and then at Tom. He followed John and stepped into the room. Another moment passed and the remaining members of the team followed them inside.

The room they entered was similar in size to the previous room. In the center was a flat white table that seemed to meld seamlessly into the white surface of the floor, as if they were one substance. On top of the table was another desiccated body, dried and shriveled. Above the body, extending down from the ceiling as though it were a part of the structure, was a huge crystalline shape of roughly the same size as the table. It had a smooth translucent surface that curved over and melded into the white surface of the walls and ceiling. On the side of the lower table were three knobs; one round, one triangular, and one square.

" Africanus?" asked John.

" By the looks of it." said Evan.

John moved slowly toward the table, finally standing before it. He reached out and touched the round knob.

" John! What are you doing?" asked Sara with exasperation.

" Just a little experiment. Don't worry. I actually have an idea about what this table does." said John.

John Philips turned the knob to the left and the crystalline structure above the body began to glow. Then an image appeared underneath, like a mirror likeness of the body on the table. But with this image they were able to see the faintly glowing picture of things inside the body. John turned the triangular knob and the image changed so that they could no longer see the outer shape of the body but instead were looking at enhanced images of its insides.

" Incredible!" said John.

John turned the third knob and the image changed hue and color.

" We're probably looking at different light spectrums. You could probably diagnose any ailment known to man with the right combination of the knobs." said John.

They all watched as John turned the knobs to varying combinations, astounded by the technology at their fingertips. Then Sara pointed to the wall behind John.

" What's that?" asked Sara.

They all turned and looked where she was pointing. On the wall behind John was a new puzzle on the wall. A flat square frame about 12 inches on a side with five smaller squares inside of it. Each of the five inner squares was a different size.

" Was that there before?" asked Evan.

" No. We would've seen it. It only appeared after I started playing with the device." said John.

John turned and got down on his knees to study the device.

" It's definitely another puzzle, or lock. More complicated than the last one. Tom, can you get a pad of paper. I want to make a drawing." said John.

Tom Merrill ran off to fetch a pad of paper.

" There's something about it that seems familiar. Some type of pattern to it. But it may take some time to work it out." said John.

Tom returned with the paper pad and John Philips began taking notes.

Dilemma

Sara and Evan sat at a table with exhaustion clearly visible in every aspect of their appearance. Sara rested her head on the table with her hands as a pillow while Evan seemed likely to fall out of his chair. They were dirty and tired. They were emotionally depleted, but more than anything else was the overriding knowledge that they were involved with something that was beyond their ability to analyze and comprehend. It drained them more than any physical exhaustion ever could. As scientists they felt powerless and impotent. Like a king without his throne.

Tom Merrill sat in a chair in a corner of the room and stared off into space. Where Sara and Evan no longer felt qualified to investigate the questions, Tom had just checked out altogether.

" What are we going to do?" asked Sara.

" I don't know Sara. Eventually we're going to have to turn it over to someone else. The question has always been when. I think we need to take the vote again." said Evan.

" When was a long time ago. We're way past the line of knowing what we're getting ourselves into." said

Sara.

"Why don't you go home and get some rest." said Evan.

"It's just afternoon. And we might solve the puzzle." said Sara.

"If he does, we'll come get you before he activates the next room." said Evan.

They heard the sound of someone shaking the outer gate and Tom got up to look through the window.

"Someone's at the outer gate." said Tom.

"Who is it." asked Evan.

"Not sure, some guy, but he's wearing a uniform." said Tom.

"The police." said Sara.

"I don't think so. Not that kind of uniform." said Tom.

"I'll go talk to him." said Evan.

Evan got up from the table and walked out the door of the field office. He approached the outer gate of the construction site but began speaking before he reached it.

"Can I help you?" asked Evan.

The man waiting at the gate wore a uniform identifying him as an employee of the local power utility. He held a metal clipboard in his hand and looked up from it to converse with Evan.

"We've been trying to track down a power short

somewhere on the system. Something's drawing a lot of juice somewhere and we've tracked it down to this location. Can you let me in so I can take a look?" said the utility worker.

Evan looked at the man for a moment, too long before answering.

" We're not using any large amounts of power here." said Evan.

" It might be a utility line on your property. Something shorting to ground. You guys are excavating in the sub-grade, you might have hit it without knowing about it. Can I come in and check it out." said the man.

" This is the Hobbs Lane tunnel project. We're just researchers doing some work at the site before the project gets going again." said Evan.

" We've been tracking this for some time now and everything looks like it's pointing to this area. Everything else is just low rise residential. It must be coming from this construction site." said the utility worker.

" I'm not sure what I can do to help you. We're not using any significant power here." said Evan.

" Can I come in and look?" asked the utility worker.

" I don't think I've got authorization to let you on to the site. I'm only supposed to let my research team have access." said Evan.

" I'm really going to need to gain access to the

property. This short's been draining the power grid for weeks. And it's only getting worse." said the man.

" I'm sorry. I really can't let you in." said Evan.

" Look pal, I can get a warrant if I have to. Do you really want me to do that?" asked the utility worker.

" I can't let you in." said Evan.

" Asshole. Don't say I didn't warn you. Next person knocking at your door's going to be a cop with a warrant." said the man.

The utility worker turned and began walking away.

" Uhmm. Excuse me." said Evan.

The utility worker stopped in mid stride and turned around.

" What?" asked the utility worker.

" How long do you think it will be before you come back with the warrant?" asked Evan.

" Are you playing games with me?" asked the man.

" No. I'm just curious about how long it might take." said Evan.

" If you make me get a warrant, and then just let me through that door when I come back . . ." said the man.

" No. I'm still not going to let you in. I'm just curious about how much time we have." interrupted Evan.

" Two or three days. We have to get an order from the judge." said the man.

" Thank you." said Evan.

" Don't mention it." said the man, before turning and walking away.

Evan returned to the field office.

" Well, we have a time limit now." said Evan.

" What do you mean?" asked Sara.

" That was a representative from the power company investigating the power outages. He says they've traced it down to this area and he wants to look around. This gives us two or three days of uninterrupted work before he comes back with a warrant. We'll have to open this to the world then. We'll have no more choice, and no more excuses." said Evan.

" Thank God. I'll be glad when it's over." said Sara.

" I'll tell John about the time limit, then I'm going home to get some sleep." said Tom.

With scarcely a word between them, the group dissipated. Each to their own home to rest. Two or three days and it would all be over for them, or so they thought.

Dreams

Evan Anderson tossed and turned in his sleep. Perspiration beaded on his upper lip and forehead. His dreams were troubled. In his dream Evan stood before the white table in the alien device and looked down on the ancient shriveled remains of the Africanus specimen. He twisted the knobs of the device and began to see a blurry indistinct image in the air space above the ancient body. He adjusted the knobs again to try and bring it into focus, working hard at the image that seemed to remain just out of reach of the twisting knobs. Finally, the image came into view but it was not the image of the Africanus specimen. He saw an image of Sara working over a table, writing something into a notebook. From behind he saw John Philips coming up behind her. John touched her neck and ran his hand down her arm. She moved to the touch, responding to his caress. He moved his face into the cradle of Sara's neck and kissed her lightly. She responded again, bringing her hand up to his face in a soft embrace. His hands embraced her waist and he pulled himself in close as he caressed her body. She turned and faced him, offering herself to him. He reached forward and hugged her. He embraced her and rubbed his hands over her body. Sara responded to him and offered her mouth to be kissed. They shared a moment of passion in Evan's dream, a dream that had turned into his nightmare.

Evan then noticed the outline of the horned beasts in the background. Indistinct shadowy figures full of menace. John Philips brought his hands up around Sara's neck and began to strangle her. At first she seemed shocked by the action but then began to realize what was happening and resisted. She pulled back from him but John had his grip firmly around her neck and continued to squeeze. They struggled against each other. Suddenly, Evan's attention was drawn to the emaciated body on the table. The ancient body turned its head to look at Evan and spoke.

" Little cheater deserved it." said the Africanus.

Evan jumped back from the body on the table and suddenly woke up in bed. He lurched to a sitting position, breathing hard and sweating from his dream. His eyes searched the room for the meaning of his nightmare. His hand came up to his chest in an effort to slow his heart.

Miles away Sara lay in her bed tossing and turning in her sleep. She threw her head back and forth. Her dreams were troubled. In her dream she saw herself in the street in front of the tunnel project. She faced the old woman. The woman beckoned for Sara to come, urged her onward with a signal of her hand. Sara hesitated, but then crossed the street and stood before her.

" I've got to show you something." said Rebecca Curtis.

" What is it?" asked Sara.

" Follow me." said Rebecca.

The old woman turned and began walking. Sara looked around and found herself in a different location. She stood in a dark alley, cold and wet. Buildings on either side were run down and abandoned, dark and neglected. Sara followed the old woman, not knowing what else to do. She followed her down into a broken out and dilapidated building, and down into a forgotten basement. She looked around.

" What do you want to show me?" asked Sara.

The old woman smiled. Suddenly, a bright light shined all around the deserted basement, with the old woman at the center. Images of the horned beasts began to appear all around the room. They flooded the basement around Sara and the old woman. Sara couldn't make out the details of how they looked but she saw flashes of gray skin and brown horns. They jumped from the light and seemed to take up position around the old woman and Sara. Suddenly the movement stopped and Sara tried to focus more closely on the demons. They remained out of focus.

" You didn't stop when I told you." said the old

woman.

Rebecca Curtis pulled out a machine gun from behind her back. She cocked the weapon and pointed it at Sara.

" Now you have to pay." said Rebecca Curtis.

" No!" said Sara, holding out her hand.

" Goodbye." said the old woman.

Rebecca Curtis pulled the trigger and a torrent of bullets flew from the gun's muzzle. Sara came awake and jumped up in her bed, her covers soaked with sweat. She looked around at the dark unknown corners of the room. She breathed in gasps and tried to calm herself. Suddenly, she heard a loud knock at the door. She jumped in her bed and waited quietly. After several minutes the loud knock came again. Filled with the terrors of her dream, Sara slowly got out of bed and pulled on a robe. She walked down the hall slowly, fearful of what might be at her door. She reached the door but didn't open it. Instead she stood by the door quietly listening. The knock came again causing Sara to jump.

" Sara!" yelled Evan from outside.

Sara recognized Evan's voice. Hesitantly, she reached forward, unlocked the door, and opened it. Evan stood outside her door, hastily dressed, hair uncombed. His face was clogged with emotion, as if he had seen or heard something that shook him to his core. His eyes were moist, but he was visibly glad to see Sara.

" Are you okay?" asked Evan.

" Yes. I think so." said Sara.

" Did you... Have a dream? A nightmare?" asked Evan.

" Yes. It was the most vivid nightmare I've ever had. What's going on Evan? Do you think it was the device?" asked Sara.

" I don't know. We're pretty far away . . . I don't know. It's hard to conceive of anything that could affect us from that distance." said Evan.

" I can't take this much longer. We have to end it. We have to tell John it's over." said Sara.

" I know." said Evan. " It's gone too far."

" What should we do?" asked Sara.

" John is still down there. He stayed late tonight to try and figure out the next cipher lock. Let's go down and talk to him." said Evan.

" What about Tom." said Sara.

"I'll call him and ask him to meet us there." said Evan.

" Okay. Give me ten minutes." said Sara.

Sara turned and entered her house.

" Sara?" said Evan.

Sara stopped and turned back to Evan.

" I had to find out if you were okay tonight. I mean, after the nightmare. It was the first thing I thought of doing. I had to know if you were okay. I had to see you." said Evan.

Sara looked down at the ground.

" It occurred to me that I can't deny this any longer." said Evan.

" Deny what?" asked Sara.

" I love you Sara. I didn't need to say it before, when time just seemed to go on forever, but now? After all that's happened. I just don't want the world to end without telling you how I feel." said Evan.

Sara's eyes became moist as she stood on the edge of charged emotion. A mix of fear, and excitement.

" I love you Sara." said Evan.

Sara came forward then and put her arms around Evan. She buried her head in his chest and squeezed tight.

" Why didn't you tell me before?" asked Sara.

" When we worked on that research project you were with John. How could I tell you then?" said Evan.

Sara merely nodded her head.

" Okay. Let's just get through this first before we talk about love. Okay." said Sara.

Evan looked at his feet for a moment and then the disciplined scientist that was his core resurfaced.

" Okay. Get ready as quick as you can." said Evan.

Sara retreated into her house.

Decision

Sara and Evan sat in the field office drinking coffee and waiting for Tom Merrill to arrive. Each seemed lost in their own thoughts, distracted, not in the moment. Lights pulled up outside the fence and they watched as Tom opened the gate, pulled his vehicle inside, and then closed it behind him. Tom ran the short distance to the field office wrapped in a warm coat and breathing puffs of breath into the cold night air. He entered the field office and shook off the cold.

" Hi Tom." said Evan.

Evan gave Tom a cup of coffee and Tom accepted it gratefully.

" What's going on?" asked Tom.

" Did you have a dream tonight, Tom? Have you had any unusual experiences? Something you might attribute to the device?" asked Evan.

" No. Maybe I've had some eerie feelings lately. But nothing like what Blake experienced." said Tom.

" Evan and I both had dreams tonight. Our dreams were different but they were both very violent in nature. Similar to what Blake described when he was working on the device." said Sara.

A moment of silence followed in which Tom tried to evaluate the situation.

" Are you thinking that the device had something to do with this?" asked Tom.

" Well . . . yes. The dreams were very intense. More intense than any other dream I've ever experienced." said Evan.

" Mine too. There must be some influence from the device. We both dreamed of the demons the old woman told us about." said Sara.

Another moment of silence.

" Look, I'm the first one who thinks that we should be turning this whole thing over to someone else. We're in way over our heads regardless of what John might think. But maybe John's right. Maybe we're all just feeling the stress over this thing. It's all we've done for the past several weeks. Day and night. With lack of sleep. With the knowledge that we're playing with something we don't understand and that might be the biggest discovery of the century. I'm not saying there aren't some weird things going on here, but I'm not ready to start blaming our dreams on this thing. Evan, what would you have said two weeks ago if I'd have told you the same story?" asked Tom.

" I'd have told you you were crazy. I'd have told you that a dream wasn't evidence." said Evan.

" Right. Take it easy. Maybe, just maybe, it was just a

normal dream. You know how sleep deprivation and stress can effect the mind." said Tom.

Another moment of silence.

" I suppose it's possible." said Evan.

" No. It's not possible. We're being affected by something in ways that we don't understand. It's real. We're not imagining this." said Sara.

" Sara, I have to admit the possibility of what Tom is saying. I'm a scientist. We just experienced it so the dream seems very real to us. But maybe it is the stress. Maybe the two aren't really connected." said Evan.

" Is John here?" asked Tom.

" No. We looked for him. He must have gone home for the night." said Evan.

" I heard back from the testing lab yesterday. The sample we took? The one of the white wall material. We got the results back." said Tom.

" What did they find?" asked Sara.

" Well, there wasn't much to work on. Most of the filings were just grit off the grinder. But the lab did think they identified something within the sample." said Tom.

" What is it?" asked Evan.

" They said that it was an organic material. They haven't identified the source, or even what the material was, but they said that it was definitely organic." said Tom.

" What does that mean?" asked Sara.

" It means that it is living, or was living, or . . ." said Tom.

" I know what organic means in this context. I mean what does it mean? That the device is organic? Are we saying that the device itself is a living organism?" asked Sara.

" It doesn't necessarily mean that. I might just be composed of organic compounds. I'm really not sure. We should talk to John." said Tom.

" Look. It's almost three in the morning now and I'm exhausted. I thought we could all talk about this but John isn't here. We can talk it over in the morning." said Evan.

" Tomorrow is the last day for us. After that, we take a vote, and we hand it over to someone else." said Sara, with a sigh of relief.

Evan grabbed his coat and moved toward the door. Sara followed instinctively.

" See you tomorrow." said Sara.

Sara grabbed her coat and walked out of the field office with Evan. Tom hung back momentarily and watched the two through the window. He was in time to see Evan take Sara's hand as they walked.

" Thought so." said Tom.

Tom looked around the room one last time, knowing that tomorrow would be their last day, and glad of it. He knew how the three of them would vote regardless of John's vote. He opened the door and walked the short distance to his car. Evan's car was slowly moving toward the gate. Tom waved and Evan waved back.

" I'll lock the gate." yelled Tom. Evan nodded his head and pulled his car out onto the street.

Tom walked toward his SUV parked just inside the gate. The street lights on Hobbs Lane began to blink intermittently. Short flashes of light that reached the tunnel project yard in brief bursts of illumination. At thirty feet away from his vehicle Tom heard the engine of his car turning over, as if the vehicle was trying to start. Fear stopped Tom in his tracks. He looked at his car and then fumbled in his pocket for the key. He pulled out his keys and looked at them. Then he looked back at the car. His car didn't have a remote start feature so what he was seeing shouldn't be possible. Was there someone inside trying to start it?

Tom took a tentative step toward his car, trying to see the darkened interior. The car engine continued to turn over but wouldn't start. He stopped. He watched in silence, unable to move. Several seconds passed and the car engine stopped turning over and became quiet. Tom waited several moments more and then took a few tentative steps toward the car. Suddenly, the front and rear running lights of his car began to flash on and off. Tom jumped involuntarily. Another moment passed and Tom took another step forward, he looked intently through the window of the car. In the bare light of the street lamp he saw no one, only an empty seat where someone should have been seated trying to start the car.

" What the hell!" said Tom.

On the other side of the field office a tractor engine began turning over, causing Tom to jump and turn around. He looked over at the tractor. The motor continued to turn over but refused to start. As he watched the whole body of the tractor began to shake and shimmy as the engine continued to turn. After several moments the engine stopped turning and the tractor was silent. Then Tom heard a noise at a small metal tool shed sitting beside the field office. The shed creaked and the metal popped and began to reverberate with movement. The shed shook and shuddered as the metal panels were pushed out from the inside. The metal expanded until it seemed that the whole shed was growing in size. Tom began to breathe rapidly. His face was contorted with fear.

A wind began to grow around the yard. Weeds and small pieces of trash were picked up and brought into the swirling mix that seemed to settle around Tom Merrill. An empty box was picked up by the wind. Tom ducked and the box passed by. Suddenly, more items began to fly in the air toward him. Boxes and bags and wood fragments were picked up by the wind and thrown in Tom's direction. Then the doors on the metal tool shed were ripped apart by the force. Tools began to fly out of the shed. Wrenches and shovels and parts began to fly toward him. Tom ducked them as best he could but he was hit by several items as they flew in his direction. Finally, he began to run for his life, moving as quickly as he could toward the open gate. The entire yard seemed to come alive in pursuit. The ground rumbled and rolled beneath his feet and everything that was not tied down now began to fly in his direction. A section of metal floor plating finally found Tom and hit him at the back of his head. He fell to the ground and didn't move again.

Yard

Sara and Evan pulled up to the tunnel project yard in Evan's car. They had stayed together the previous night and there was now a closeness between them that didn't exist before. A warmth and passion in the small looks that they shared. They hadn't discussed it, but they both knew instinctively that it wasn't the time to let others know about the new status of their relationship. The issues before them were too meaningful and far-reaching to allow potential distractions. It was likely that they might guess that things had changed, but Sara and Evan wouldn't talk about it.

Sara jumped out of the car to unlock the gate. She reached for the lock but noticed that the padlock wasn't in place. The gate was unlocked. She wondered for a moment, but then merely opened the gate the rest of the way so Evan could pull his car inside. Sara noticed Tom's car in the yard in the same position she had last seen it. John Philips' car was now parked next to Tom's. Evan exited his car and walked up to Sara who seemed not to notice his presence.

" Tom's car is in the same spot it was when we left him last night." said Sara.

" It doesn't mean anything. Tom parks in the same spot everyday." said Evan.

" I suppose so." said Sara.

" John's here. Let's go find him." said Evan.

Evan locked the front gate of the construction yard and took Sara's hand. Sara allowed herself to be pulled toward the tunnel entrance by the tender insistence of Evan's hand. Her night with Evan had left her feeling relaxed and at ease for the first time in weeks, but now there was something edging at the dread in her heart. Something visceral and innate that she couldn't pin down. She felt that something was wrong. They had always been in over their heads, but now she felt that they had gone too far and that there was now no way of turning back. It was a feeling she had, though nothing she saw was evidence beyond Tom's car and an unlocked gate.

Evan and Sara walked down the tunnel ramp and down into the artifact where John was already at work. He sat before the cipher lock in the second room. He turned his head momentarily as the two entered.

" Hi. I got here early. Had an inspiration in the middle of the night." said John.

" You've solved it?" asked Evan excitedly.

" I think so. I'll know in a moment. You see, this lock is really about proportion as opposed to color matching like the last lock. Ever heard of the golden ratio?

The divine proportion? It's a ratio. One point one six one? It appears

in art, science, nature, architecture. They've even associated it with the physics of black holes. Negative specific heat. Well, moving these squares in the right combination creates the same magic proportion in a sort of cascading effect that we've seen throughout all of history. Since written history began." said John.

" Have you seen Tom?" asked Sara.

" No. His car was here when I pulled in this morning. He left the gate unlocked as well." said John.

" The gate was unlocked when you came in?" asked Sara.

" Yes. I haven't seen him yet this morning." said John.

" John, we need to talk about things before you open the next lock." said Evan.

" Too late." said John.

John moved the last square piece into place and then stood back. The cipher lock seemed to vibrate in place for a moment and then disappeared. It was simply absorbed into the wall. The wall itself then opened down its center, splitting apart and creating a door opening in the center of the wall. John moved back away from the opening. Sara and Evan were startled but they kept their positions. Slowly, John moved forward and peeked his head through the new opening.

" It's okay. Come inside." said John.

John cautiously stepped through the newly created doorway followed by Sara and Evan. They looked around reverently. Like entering a cathedral or sanctuary. They felt the veneration of treading on hallowed ground.

The space they entered was similar to the previous rooms, except for a large platform at the back end that spanned the entire width of the room. The platform had two steps that stepped down to the floor level of the room. The back wall beyond the platform consisted of the same type of crystal like material they had noted at the analysis table in the last room.

" Evan, I don't like this." said Sara.

" Just don't touch anything." said Evan.

" What are we looking at?" asked Sara.

" I'm not sure." said John, studying the platform and crystal wall as he spoke.

" It's a stage or something." said Evan.

" A platform. But look at the back wall. Something's going to happen with that wall." said John.

" But what?" asked Sara.

" I've been thinking about this. About the whole thing. What we've seen and what we've been through. I think I know what this is all about." said John.

" Well, don't keep it a secret." said Evan.

" We know that the machine, or device, or ship, whatever it is. Is interested in humans. We think it's been running the same program since it first picked up our shriveled friends. Each room has taken some level of intelligence to open. And each room has taken a greater degree of intelligence. The rooms are screening for something. Intelligence. We're not meant to move on to the next room until we've reached a certain level of evolution. Until we are advanced enough to earn it. It's like an intelligence test. But with a much greater purpose." said John.

" What's the purpose?" asked Sara.

" It's no game. Whoever put this device here has a purpose. And that involves us. Not just humans, but evolved humans. Intelligent humans. Humans whose minds are developed enough to include color differentiation and organization. Developed enough to be able to discern complex spatial relations. These are filters. The device knows what it's looking for and it won't let us proceed unless we meet its standards." said John.

" It's testing us?" asked Sara.

John merely nodded his head.

" The problem is why? It's taken an incredible level of technology to put this here. That means it must have some incredible purpose. Something that would warrant the effort." said John.

" Is this wall just another test? Is there something here to solve?" asked Evan.

" What's on the other side?" asked Sara.

" I'm not sure. But for the first time I'm beginning to think we shouldn't find out." said John.

" What do you mean?" asked Evan.

" Look, I'm driven by this stuff. Science, exploration, analysis. It's what I live for. But I'm scared. We're into something that I can't even guess about. With wild and totally unpredictable consequences. Maybe it's not a question of turning it over to the government to investigate. Maybe it's a question of should anyone investigate this." said John.

" What are you suggesting?" asked Sara.

" I don't know." said John.

" Well, short of blowing this thing up there's not much we can do. The genie is already out of the bottle." said Sara.

Gate

A utility truck pulled up to the tunnel project gate followed by a dark gray sedan and a police car. The truck parked on the street in front of the gate. The sedan and the police cruiser parked behind the truck. The same utility worker, who had previously demanded entry, exited the truck from the driver's side. A man wearing a suit and tie exited from the sedan.

The two men could not have contrasted more. The utility worker wore coveralls, muscular, with a tanned and bearded visage. The lawyer who accompanied him was pale and pristine, with glasses and shiny shoes that were covered with dust almost immediately. Two officers exited the police car and joined the two at the gated entrance.

" I hope you're right about this." said the Lawyer.

" Don't worry. This is the place. The grid is being sucked dry and it's coming from this location." said the utility worker.

" Okay gentlemen. Let's serve a warrant and see what's inside." said Officer Moore.

Officer Moore walked up to the gate and examined the lock and chain.

" This is easy." said the officer.

" You going to break it?" asked the lawyer.

" Hey! Anyone here? Police. Open the gate." yelled Officer Moore.

The police officer shook the gate and looked over the yard.

" Open up. Police." yelled the officer.

Platform

Sara, Evan, and John stood in front of the platform in the third room of the artifact. The crystal wall drew their attention to the point of obsession. They couldn't stop looking at it, even when talking.

" You think this thing's dangerous?" asked Evan.

" I'm not sure. I'd feel a lot better if I could figure out why it was put here." said John.

" Maybe it's some kind of communication device. Maybe it's

trying to make sure we're smart enough to be able to use it." said Sara.

" But it's been sitting here for over a million years. Would you be that patient just to talk to us? Whoever they are, they're probably dead by now." said Evan.

" Maybe the device doesn't know it's been a million years." said Sara.

" And maybe it doesn't care. Maybe it knows that that much time has passed but it doesn't matter." said John.

" Are you saying that whoever is waiting to hear from us has been waiting patiently for a million years?" said Evan.

" No. But maybe time itself is not a problem. Maybe it

communicates across time. Maybe when this thing does what it's supposed to do, it will have been just a few days for the people who built it. Maybe its function is to bridge not only space, but time." said John.

" That's some pretty wild speculation." said Evan.

" I'm just trying to find something that fits the facts. Scientific theory. In this case, we know what the facts are, but we need to formulate a theory to fit those facts. Then we can make intelligent decisions." said John.

" A decision? A decision about what? There is no decision. We're turning this over to the authorities." said Sara.

" Maybe the old woman was right. Maybe we never should have
disturbed this place." said Evan.

Officer Lewis pulled a bolt cutter from the rear of the patrol car and joined Officer Moore at the gate. The utility worker and lawyer merely looked on with interest.

" Okay. My throat is getting horse. I'm done yell'in." said Officer Moore.

" We didn't serve the warrant." said the utility worker.

" No one to serve it too. We'll have to go in to serve it on someone." said Officer Lewis.

Officer Moore broke the chain with the cutters and the gate swung open. The bolt cutter was dropped to the ground and the officers walked into the construction yard followed by the utility worker and the lawyer. They walked to the field office and Officer Moore knocked on the door.

" Hello. Police. Please open the door." yelled Officer Moore.

" They're probably gone by now. I told him when I'd be coming back." said the utility worker.

Officer Lewis surveyed the building itself, walking around the exterior and looking for other points of entry.

He was stopped by a pile of trash and debris that lay piled up against the building at the rear. He probed the surface of the pile with his foot and noticed a shoe lying just under a section of corrugated tin roofing. He reached forward and pulled the corrugated roofing away to reveal what was beneath. The body of Tom Merrill lay nestled in the pile of trash.

" Holy shit! We've got a body here. There's a body under the trash." yelled Officer Lewis.

Officer Moore ran to the side of the building and joined his partner.

" Holy shit! This man's been beaten to death." said Officer Moore.

Both Officers drew their service weapons in response.

" We're not serving a warrant anymore gentlemen. This just turned into a crime scene." said Officer Moore.

" I'll call for backup." said Officer Lewis.

Officer Lewis pulled his radio mic from his shoulder and keyed it.

" The radio isn't working. It's dead." said Officer Lewis.

Officer Moore keyed his mic with the same result.

" Okay, you drive back to the station and get backup out here, asap." said Officer Moore.

Officer Lewis ran to the patrol car and tried to start

it. Nothing happened. The motor wouldn't turn over and the radio was dead. He got out of the car.

" No radio. No lights. Nothing." yelled Officer Lewis.

The lawyer pulled out his mobile phone.

" I've got nothing. It won't even turn on." said the lawyer.

Several moments passed in which the police officers seemed at a loss for options. No training they had ever received included this scenario.

" Okay. Let's see what we've got here. Then we'll walk back to the station if we have to." said Officer Moore.

The two police officers surveyed the exterior of the site but ended up at the ramp that led down into the main dig site of the Hobbs Lane Tunnel Project. The site appeared deserted, but they were taking no chances.

" You two stand back." said Officer Moore.

The utility worker and the lawyer remained at the tunnel entrance.

With guns drawn the two officers proceeded past the boring equipment until they stood in front of the device itself.

" What is that thing?" asked Officer Lewis.

" I've never seen anything like it." said Officer Moore.

" This must be the drain on the grid." said Officer

Lewis.

" Yeah, but what is it?" asked Officer Moore.

They walked slowly to the entrance of the device. Voices could be heard from within.

" I hear something. People talking." said Officer Moore.

The two police officers entered the device cautiously, leaving the utility worker and lawyer looking on from the entrance to the tunnel. The voices they heard were muffled, but constant. Both kept their weapons drawn.

Sara and Evan were standing side by side when the officers moved up slowly behind them through the opening of the third room. John stood slightly ahead of them, studying the crystalline structure of the wall beyond the platform. None of them were aware of the police officers presence until they spoke.

" Ok. This is the police. Everyone down on your knees. Now!" yelled Officer Moore.

Sara, Evan, and John turned in unison. The intrusion by the armed officers seemed incongruous to the point of farce. Like a painted clown demanding attention at a funeral service.

" What are you doing here?" asked Evan.

" On your knees. Do you hear me? We found your friend outside." said Officer Moore.

" Tom! Is he okay?" asked Sara.

" Oh yeah. He's fine. He stopped breathing a couple of hours ago but other than that he's fine." said Officer Lewis.

" He's dead?" asked John.

" Yes, death usually follows when you stop breathing. This is the last time I'm going to ask you. Get on your knees and put your hands above your head." said Officer Lewis.

Officer Moore brought his gun up higher and sighted down it's barrel.

" You don't understand. This isn't what you think." said Evan.

" We'll get it sorted out down at the station." said Officer Moore.

" We can't do that. You don't understand what we've found here. It's the biggest discovery of the century. We have to turn it over to the authorities." said John.

A flickering light danced across the crystal wall surface behind John Phillips. Evan and Sara both turned to observe it.

" What I do understand is that if you don't get on your knees and put your hands over your head I'm going to have to shoot you in the leg." said Officer Moore.

The light flashed across the wall again. Multicolored, a random pattern of light crossing the surface from one side to the other.

At the top of the ramp the utility worker could

faintly hear voices coming from the device.

" What's going on down there?" said the utility worker.

" We were told to wait here." said the Lawyer.

" I know." said the utility worker. " But what if somethings going on down there? Maybe we should try and help."

" Help with what? Just let the cops handle this." said the attorney.

The lights in the tunnel dimmed with the loss of power. They flickered several times and then finally went out altogether. The Utility worker ran to the top of the ramp and surveyed the street.

" I think the whole city is out this time." said the utility worker.

Inside the device, Officer Moore held his weapon pointed at John Phillips. The look on his face was serious and deliberate.

" I'm going to tell you one more time. On your knees mister." said the police officer.

" Wait." said John.

Officer Moore fired a warning shot to the corner of the room. The bullet ricocheted off of the wall surface and hit the crystal wall. A flash occurred, and the whole crystal wall lit up. The dancing light now moved and fluctuated over the entire surface of the wall. Brilliant colors and patterns emerged as the light jumped and fluttered across the crystal pallet. John turned around and noticed the light for the first time. The two police officers stared as if entranced.

" Of course. The last test. Weapons." said John.

The light seemed to take on more substance now, as a pattern emerged to the illumination on the crystal wall. Now the light took the form of images. A reflection of something they were seeing beyond the wall. As if the wall separated two spaces with a translucent film. A pulsing sound began to reverberate throughout the room. The sound was so rhythmic and powerful that Sara could feel it to the core of her body. She covered her ears and fell to the ground. She tried to make sense of what she was seeing but the sound and the light seemed to alter her perceptions, or alter reality, she couldn't be sure which. The light seemed to meld and run, sometimes seeming not to be bound by the limits of the wall surface. She looked at John and Evan and noticed that their very substance seemed to reverberate with the sound. The two police officers seemed frozen in place, also reverberating with the sound and the light.

Sara couldn't take her eyes away from the spectacle taking place before her. The lights on the wall grew sharper and more distinct. Then a light flashed brightly in the center of the wall and a creature jumped through from the light and into the room before them. Its skin was a dull gray paste, almost translucent. It was bipedal, but there the resemblance ended. Its head was strangely triangular in shape with the chin ending in a distinct point. Horns protruded upward from each side of the head. The mouth was oversize with brown bony mandibles at either side. The eyes were the most human part of the face, having the same depth and intelligence she associated with humans. The body of the creature was smooth skinned, but along the back of both the arms and legs were brown spiny ridges, and on the end of each arm was an angular hand with three spiny fingers and an opposable thumb. The demon of her nightmares.

The creature looked around the room quickly and settled its gaze on the three scientists. I raised its hand in a gesture that would have been synonymous with the tipping of one's hat. John was stunned and horrified at the clear recognition and sign of gratitude from the alien. What had they done?

The Alien then turned its gaze to the police officers who stood transfixed from what they had witnessed. At that moment the wall flashed again and two more creatures, looking identical to the first, jumped through the wall. The original creature looked at Officer Moore purposefully. The officer lowered his gun. His face took on a strange look of pain or intense pressure. His whole body became rigid and stiff.

" This is bad." said John.

John crawled across the floor and grabbed Sara and Evan by the arm. He began pulling them out of the room. The two moved slowly, trying to break the hypnotic effect of the scene playing out before them.

" We've got to go." said John.

John pulled them to the next room and they were able to stand. John continued to pull and they began to move more quickly. They exited the artifact and found the utility worker and lawyer standing outside.

" What's going on in there?" asked the utility worker.

" You've got to get out." said John.

" Where are the two policemen?" asked the lawyer.

" We can talk about this outside. We've got to move." said John.

John began to move toward the ramp but was restrained by the hand of the utility worker.

" You're not going anywhere. What did you do to the two police officers?" asked the utility worker.

John forcibly shoved the man's hand from his arm.

" Something is happening in there. I don't have time to explain it but you've got to get out." said John.

The lawyer pulled the utility worker back with a hand on his shoulder.

" Let them go." said the lawyer.

John pulled Sara and Evan toward the ramp. Half way up Sara stopped.

" Where are we going?" asked Sara.

" Away from here." said John.

" Those were aliens." said Evan.

" No kidding. And the machine they sent here did its job. They're coming through." said John.

" But what do they want?" asked Sara.

" Look. This is just a guess but look at your own dreams. Look at what the old woman told you. I don't think they built that machine so they could come through and have a friendly chat. I think this is an invasion." said John.

" But they didn't have any weapons." said Evan.

" I don't think they need them." said John.

John looked back and noticed that the utility worker and lawyer were no longer visible.

" What are we going to do now?" asked Evan.

" I'm not sure. But whatever we decide to do we should do it out of here." said John.

Evan looked down at the device and saw the lawyer emerge from the door. In a way that was hard to define, he no longer looked human. His face was flat, emotionless, devoid of any signs of personality or humanity. His movements were stiff and directed, like that of a machine rather than a human being.

" Something's wrong." said Evan.

Sara and John looked at where Evan's gaze directed

them and they saw the lawyer standing there looking at them. The lawyer took several steps toward them and stopped. Then the whole space around them seemed to erupt with movement. The festoon lighting at the tunnel walls began to jump and move. Tools and instruments begin to shake and move on the floor or tables where they sat. Some of the smaller tools began to lift into the air and fly in the direction of the three scientists. Then all of the debris in the room began to fly in the air around them.

" Run!" yelled John.

The three ran up the ramp as the maelstrom of flying debris followed behind them. Evan turned his head as he reached the upper door on the ramp and saw twenty of the alien creatures flooding out of the device doorway. The three stumbled out into the construction yard of the Hobbs Lane tunnel project. Breathing hard and sweating from exertion.

" Where do we go?" asked Evan.

" The field office." said John.

Sara, John, and Evan ran to the field office and entered, closing the door behind them. Evan stood with his back against the door, breathing hard. John bent over with his hands on his knees and Sara sat down in a chair.

" What now?" asked Sara.

" I'm not sure." said John.

" Lets call the police." said Sara.

Sara pulled out her cell phone and attempted to make a call.

" My battery is dead." said Sara.

Evan reached for his phone.

" Mine too." said Evan.

Sara ran to the land phone on the field desk and picked it up. She held the receiver to her ear, but put it down after only a moment.

" Nothing. No signal." said Sara.

Evan flipped the light switch several times but nothing happened.

" The power is out everywhere. Landlines, portable devices, everything." said Evan.

" What's happening? How could the device do that?" asked Sara.

" Something we don't understand. They can pull power from the devices around them. Enough power to disable those devices." said John.

" In the tunnel, you said something about the final test, what did you mean?" asked Evan.

" Weapons. Violence. Weapons of violence. Do we have it within us to kill, to use violence against each other.

"What?" asked Evan.

" Don't you see. They're screening for mental characteristics. You saw what happened down there. It wasn't the creatures who were making things fly around down in the tunnel. It was the lawyer. It was a human being. That's what they're looking for. A mind developed enough to be useful to them. A mind that can be altered. A mind that can be turned into something else. That they can use as soldiers. They could never

take over the earth by themselves. Not against billions of humans. They need to convert us. They need to use us. Make us work for them. Make slaves of us." said John.

" You think they want to enslave us?" said Sara.

" We don't know anything for certain. But the portal didn't open until that policeman shot the gun." said John.

" We better get out of here." said Sara.

Evan moved to the window and looked out.

" Something's going on down there." said Evan.

" What's happening?" asked John.

" I don't know. But I can see the outer door to the ramp and there's a green light pulsing down there." said Evan.

" What could they be doing?" asked Sara.

" I don't know. And I'm not sure I want to stay around to find out." said John.

" We should head to town. We've got to warn people. We need to tell the police. Activate the national guard." said Sara.

" We should never have dug that thing up." said Evan.

" Too late for that now. Sara's right. We have to warn people. This is a problem for the military now." said John.

Station

Evan opened the door of the field office and looked cautiously in the direction of the entrance to the tunnel project. A green glow seemed to emanate indistinctly from the interior. Another moment passed and he ran from the field office followed by Sara and John. They headed for the car where Evan opened the door and jumped into the driver's seat. He tried to start the car but nothing happened. No starter, no clicking, no lights, nothing. John ran to his car with the same result. Evan and Sara, feeling exposed, ran for cover behind John's car. They peeked over the hood of the car at the tunnel building and ramp. Strange lights could be seen pulsating inside, along with a deep vibrating sound of something unseen and unimagined.

" What do we do now?" asked Sara.

" Anything that uses electrical power is disabled. Including vehicles. We run. Straight to the police." said Evan.

" The police station is miles away." said Sara.

" What choice do we have?" asked Evan.

They exchanged looks for a moment, then John stood up and ran toward the open gate of the construction yard.

Evan grabbed Sara's hand and followed. He looked back for a moment as he ran and saw the utility worker standing by the entrance to the tunnel. Small objects and debris swirled around him in the air like a miniature storm.

" Run." yelled Evan.

Evan looked back again and the utility worker was still standing in the same place. Something about his stance and the blank stare on his face told Evan that he was not the same. The swarm of objects and debris floating in the air around him began to move toward the three scientists. John was through the gate and reversed his momentum, ready to close the gate when Evan and Sara came through. Evan and Sara came through the gate and John swung the gate closed. In the next moment the gate was pelted by small tools and objects from the construction yard.

" That was close." said Evan.

" Let's keep moving." said John.

The three scientists ran. When they had traversed a half a block they saw Rebecca Curtis standing purposefully at the side of the road. Nothing on earth could have slowed their pace and drawn their attention except that one old woman. They slowed their pace but kept walking past her.

" Now you've done it haven't you? I told you not to dig. I told you what would happen. And now it's too late. You've cursed us all. All of humanity will pay for your avarice and stupidity. The demons have been unleashed now, and it's your fault. You set them free!" yelled Rebecca Curtis in a tirade.

Evan and Sara couldn't look the woman in the eyes. With faces downcast they continued on past her. Leaving her behind to rant and wail her reprisal of a warning not heeded.

It took them an hour to traverse to the center of town. They were dirty, tired, and sore. As they reached the town center it became obvious that the power outage was widespread. Cars had stopped in the middle of the street and would no longer start. Traffic lights had stopped working. People were walking and milling about on the street. No one had an explanation for what was happening to their town, but panic had not yet set in. Most people anticipated the return of power, and normalcy. Their talk and lack of hysteria seemed out of place with what the scientists had just witnessed. They watched absently as the scientists passed by. Sara, Evan, and John could only stare back blankly, knowing more than they would dare to admit.

" How do you say this? We can't just start screaming that there's an alien invasion. They'll lock us up." said Sara.

" It does seem a little strange and surreal somehow." said John.

" We've got to take this to the police. Somehow contact the military." said Evan.

" I'm not sure how far the power draw extends, but

it's pretty obvious that it's at least this far." said John.

" The Police Station is just another block up on Third." said Sara.

The three began running again, watched by the crowd in the streets.

" There's an invasion coming. You better run." yelled Evan randomly.

The people standing at the sidewalk didn't react, but merely looked on as the three continued down the road.

" They didn't believe me." said Evan.

" We did this Evan. God only knows what's going to happen now." said John.

" We did, but we're also going to be the ones to stop it. The old lady is right. It's our fault. And it won't walk away from our culpability." said Evan. " We're going to fix it."

Truth or Lie

The three scientists entered the Police Station to find a department in complete confusion and disarray. The officers wandered and moved about purposefully, but nothing that they touched worked. Their entire way of life was dependent on the power they so gleefully ignored. Despite their intentions, all they could do was test the equipment and report back on the non-operable status. Even the emergency generator and flashlights wouldn't function, and by the end of the day they would be in total darkness.

Evan, Sara, and John, stood in the front lobby of the small Police Station watching the anarchy of an organization robbed of its power. They caught their breath after the strenuous journey from the tunnel project. Sara sat in one of the chairs along the side of the lobby and John bent down with his hands on his knees. Evan was the first to recover. He walked up to the receptionist desk with a purposeful stride.

" We need to speak to someone immediately." said Evan.

" You are speaking to someone." said the

receptionist.

" We need to report an attack. An invasion. Up at the tunnel project. It's what's causing all the blackouts." said Evan.

" Look, nothing is working right now so I can take a written report and that's about it." said the receptionist.

" I know. We know what's causing blackouts and power outages throughout the City. That's what we want to report." said Evan.

" Our phones are out too." said the receptionist. " All I can do is take a written report."

Evan slammed his fist down on the desk. The receptionist jumped in her seat.

" We need to speak to someone now! It's very important." said Evan.

The woman was silent for a moment before saying simply, " Just a moment."

The receptionist got up from her desk and walked to the back office area. A moment later she returned with a tall heavy set Police Officer in uniform.

" Can I help you?" asked the Sergeant.

" Yes. We've come from the Hobbs Lane tunnel project. Something was dug up out there. Something in the ground. Creatures started coming out of it. They took over two police officers and two people from the electric company. You've got to call the military." said Evan.

The Sergeant looked at him doubtfully.

" Look, we've got a lot on our plate right now. As you can see we're a little busy trying to figure things out." said the Sergeant.

" Yes. And we know what's causing all of this. We dug something up at the tunnel project. It's sucking power from the grid." said Evan.

" You dug something up? What did you dig up?" asked the Sergeant.

" It's very hard to explain, we're not entirely sure, but these things started coming out of it. They have technology that allows them to suck power from our power grid. That's why the power is out everywhere. You've got to get a hold of the military as quickly as you can." said Evan.

" Well, right now we're having a hard time getting a hold of anyone, and I do mean anyone. Nothing is working at the moment." said the Sergeant.

" Look, there are creatures that came out of this thing, you understand? I'm talking about aliens here. And they're mobilizing as we speak. God knows how many have come through by now." said Evan.

" Creatures? What kind of creatures?" asked the Sergeant.

" Aliens. Aliens, damn it. They're aliens coming up from the ground. Not from the sky, they're coming out of the ground!" said Evan.

Silence.

" Look. I know how this sounds but you've got to believe what I'm saying." said Evan.

Sara walked up to the desk.

" He's telling the truth. We're scientists. From the University. We were out there doing some research when we found this thing in the ground, this device. We're not really sure what it is, but a portal opened and now there are aliens coming through it. Real aliens." said Sara.

John Philips sat in one of the chairs and cringed at how they sounded.

" It's true. As crazy as this sounds, it's true." said Sara.

" You've got to evacuate the town. And you need reinforcements. You need the military or the National Guard." said Evan.

The Sergeant shifted his weight slowly.

" We've got aliens coming out of the ground at the tunnel project?" asked the Sergeant.

Evan nodded his head vigorously.

" You realize that you both sound about as crazy as you can get. Crazy except that I can't reach my two officers who were sent out there this morning. And we haven't got a communication device in the whole City that's working. I've even got a couple of bike patrols out there and I can't reach them either. The cars won't work, the radios won't work, and the powers off everywhere. So as much as I'd like to call it crazy, and get on with my day, I'm looking for an explanation of what's happening out there. So far, yours is the only one I've got." said the Sergeant.

" It's the device. It's responsible for the power outage. It can somehow pull power from the electrical grid, and from cars and radios. We don't know how, or how far away. But there's no doubt of it." said Evan.

" We've seen it. They can disable our power systems . . . draw power from the grid and use it for their own use. They can suck power from everything around them." said Sara.

" Okay. I'm going to send a couple of officers on foot over to the tunnel station just on the off chance that something's happening out there. The very off chance that there's something in your statements. In the meantime, why don't you three wait here until we know what's going on." said the Sergeant.

" Those were my thoughts exactly." said Evan.

Waiting

Evan paced the floor of the police station lobby. His mind raced with the implications of what they had seen, but mostly with the things they could only imagine. What was happening at the tunnel project? Their power systems were so primary to the function of life that taking away that one thing made everything else collapse. Were they really that vulnerable? Were they really that weak? It had been hours and the power was still off. No communication had been made. No one had returned from the site. When darkness came they would be reduced to the stone age. Lighting fires and candles for light and heat. Looming in the back of his mind was the thought that they were responsible. They had brought this on, just as the old woman had said. They had caused this calamity. They had kept going in hubris and presumption of supremacy. How could a million year old device hold any threat? How they had failed. That thought was like a weight that threatened to overpower his sagacity. Yet it was also a driving force, Evan was determined to undo what they had done.

Sara and John sat on the chairs on either side and

watched Evan pace. Evan's impatience showed in the character of his stride. Finally, he approached the secretary.

" When are we going to know something? It's been hours." said Evan.

" Sir, we're doing the best we can. All we can do is wait for the officers to report in. We have no communication once they walk out that front door. The three officers that the Sergeant sent haven't reported back." said the receptionist.

" When do we stop waiting and do something? We've got to notify the military." said Evan.

" Let me get the Sergeant." said the receptionist.

The receptionist got up from her chair but the Sergeant was already walking to the front counter.

" We're still waiting, Sir. I'll let you know when someone checks in." said the Sergeant.

" We can't wait for that. They may never be coming back. You've got to contact someone who can respond in force." said Evan.

" And how would you propose I do that? There's not a car, truck, rail car, or anything else running for God knows how far. There's not a phone, cell phone, radio, TV, or any other electronic device working that we can locate. The next precinct is ten miles from here and I've got an officer walking to that precinct now. I've got a total of 12 men on shift right now and I can't contact any of them once they walk out that door. What else is it you think I should be doing at this moment?" asked the Sergeant, clearly annoyed.

" Then we've got to evacuate the City. Get everyone out of here until we can figure out what's going on." said Evan.

" And how do you propose I contact the hundred thousand people in this City? Loud speaker? Public address system? They're all out." said the Sergeant.

Evan turned from the Sergeant and walked away. Dumb struck by the sheer magnitude of their reliance on technology. The Sergeant retreated to the back office.

" We're wasting our time. We shouldn't be waiting here any

Longer." said John.

" Maybe we should make the trip to the next Police Station ourselves? At least then we might figure out how far the power drain extends." said Sara.

Evan walked up to the glass store front of the building and peered out. He looked for several moments staring down the street in the direction of the tunnel project.

" Someone's coming." said Evan.

Sara and John walked up to the glass front of the building.

" Looks like a police officer." said Evan.

They saw a woman in police uniform running down the street from the direction of the tunnel project. She passed pedestrians on the street who watched her pass with some trepidation visible on their faces. She ran into the station and paused to catch her breath. Her uniform appeared disheveled and her hair had fallen out of the bun on the top of her head. She had blood flowing lightly down one arm.

" What's happening out there?" asked Evan.

" Sergeant!" yelled the police woman.

The Sergeant ran out to the front lobby area.

" Are you alright?" asked the Sergeant.

" Yea. I got hit by a piece of flying glass but other than that I'm okay." said Leah.

" What's happening out there? We haven't heard a word from anyone in hours." asked the Sergeant.

" The radios are still out. And I haven't seen another uniform out there so I can't tell you what happened to the others." said Leah.

" What's going on?" asked the Sergeant.

" They're right Sarg. Either there are groups of aliens moving down the street or these are some of the best costumes I've ever seen." said Leah.

" You saw aliens?" asked the Sergeant.

Sara and Evan exchanged looks. Leah continued but was on the edge of hysteria with each sentence.

" Yea. And they're coming this way. They travel with a group of humans in front of them. The

people have this power that no one should have.
They use the things around them as weapons. They
can pick things up with their minds and send them
flying at you. I saw several people taken out this
way. I tried to shoot but my pistol was ripped from
my hand." said Leah.

Evan heard the sound of a crash from outside and ran
to the window.

" My God. Come look." said Evan.

Sara and John ran to the glass. The Sergeant and Leah
came up behind them. They looked out on a scene that took
them several moments to comprehend. Several hundred feet
down the road they saw a small group of people running down
the street toward the police station. They were being assaulted.
Hit by objects thrown by some unseen force. Cut by shards of
glass picked up in the maelstrom that followed them. Debris
and dirt flew in patterns of whirling intensity, driven without
effort by a line of humans that followed them. The humans
that followed appeared different. They were rigid and stiff.
Moving without emotion or feeling, without character or
recognition. They walked purposefully and methodically down
the street. Hunting those running before them with an alien
force.

The line of humans circled back on each side,
enveloping two aliens who appeared to be in control of them.
The aliens at the center of the circle seemed to watch all that

happened around them. Periodically, an alien would look in one direction or another and the humans on that side would turn to look as well. The aliens wore half helmets that covered the back of their heads and extended to the top. Armor plates covered the backs of their arms and legs and they carried a small metallic backpack on their back. As they watched from the Police Station window the group saw a small metal rod rise out of the backpack and spray a circular pattern of thick liquid over the body of the alien.

" What was that?" asked Sara.

" I don't know. Maybe something related to the climate they come from?" said John.

The crowd of people running from the alien cohort seemed to be dwindling. A woman fell behind the others and was tripped by a trash bag that flew into her path. She fell to the street and a maelstrom of debris was directed against her as she struggled to regain her footing. She stumbled, was cut by shards of glass and hit by rocks and pieces of debris. She fell again and didn't move. The line of humans moved slowly, stepping over the bodies of those they had killed in their methodical march down the street. Evan, Sara, and the others watched the scene playing out before them with shock and confusion.

" They're coming up every street like that. Every street that's running North/South has a group like this. They tear it up. They're tearing the city apart. It looks like a war zone." said Leah.

" Evan, we should do something." said Sara.

" What do you want to do?" asked John.

" I'll show you what I'm going to do." said the Sergeant.

The Sargent ran to the back of the station and disappeared. The receptionist stepped slowly up to the glass and watched the scene unfold with her mouth wide open and a face pale with fear. Everyone lined up against the glass front of the building and watched with fascination and terror. Unable to move from the site, and unable to act. The Sergeant came out from the back of the station carrying a shotgun in his hands. He was followed by another officer who also carried a shotgun.

" Stay here." said the Sergeant.

The Sergeant barked his command without stopping. He ran out into the street and took a position behind a police car in front of the station. The other officer ran to the other side of the street and took up position. The three scientists, the receptionist, and Leah the police woman watched in silence from inside the station. It was as if the whole of the world was suspended while the scene played itself out. No one could move and no one could talk. They watched with fear and terror threatening to overcome their minds.

When the group was within fifty feet of the Police Sergeant's position he took aim and fired at a man in the line.

The man took the shot in the stomach but kept moving. The Sergeant took another shot hitting the man square in the chest. The man faltered and tripped, finally going down without appearing to feel pain at any time. The Sergeant took aim at the alien behind the line but the human line of protection closed and he hit another man in the shoulder. A similar scene played itself out with the other officer on the other side of the street, and the maelstrom reached them. The Sergeant took another shot at the man standing in front of the alien but the barrel of the gun was blown to the side and he missed his target. Debris began to hit him and he narrowly ducked a bike handle bar that twisted through the air in his direction. Glass began to cut him on his arm and neck and the police car began to shake violently. A toilet seat hit him in the head and he went down.

The Sergeant looked across the road and saw his fellow officer standing on the sidewalk watching him. The officer looked different, no fear of the oncoming crowd of humans, and no debris touched him. He was converted. The Sergeant looked on for a moment with sad eyes, trying to shield himself from the maelstrom of force around him. A rock crushed his leg and he screamed with pain. Then a tire iron hit him in the head and he went quiet. The police car adjacent to him shuddered and shook violently and finally rolled over on top of him, ending the scene.

The remaining officer joined the crowd of humans

surrounding the alien, taking the place of the one shot by the Sergeant, and they moved forward again, stepping over and around the bodies and debris in their path.

As the alien force approached, the group at the window backed away from the glass. They stared in complete silence from positions farther back in the station as the group of humans with their alien controllers passed by. As the alien passed before the glass of the station it stopped and looked over at the group inside. It stayed there for several moments looking at them and not moving. The receptionist moved back further into the station and covered her mouth. As if having mercy on them, the alien finally moved forward again, taking the crowd of humans down the street.

" I think we should get out of here." said Sara.

She looked around and noticed that the receptionist was gone and that the station appeared deserted with the exception of her, Evan, John, and Leah.

" I think you're right." said Evan.

" But where to?" asked John.

" The next police station. The next closest police station." said Sara.

" It's down on tenth street." said Leah.

" Will you come with us?" asked Evan.

" There's not much I can do here. Lets get going." said Leah.

Flight

After the aliens and their controlled humans had passed, Evan opened the front door of the Police Station and looked out in either direction. He moved out onto the road followed by Sara, John, and Leah. They made their way to a side street and worked their way through town, checking the intersections for other groups of controlled humans. The streets and buildings they passed were in ruins. Broken glass, light poles that had been knocked over, debris littered throughout the street. The City that had been so familiar to them just hours before was now strange and unrecognizable. They had taken everything for granted in their world made of shadows, now they ran down the street like frightened children in a world turned upside down. On Second street they ran across the intersection only to find themselves merged with a group of people fleeing from a controlled group of humans and two alien controllers. They turned and ran with the group, trying to make it to another side street. A heavy set man tripped in front of Sara and she tripped over him, hitting the pavement hard. Evan saw her and Stopped.

" John!" yelled Evan loudly.

John and Leah stopped and ran back to help Evan. The heavy set man got up and stumbled forward again into a run. Sara took Evan's hand and pulled herself up. Behind them the line of humans preceded by a swirling storm of debris came forward. The debris started to flow around them. Evan pulled at Sara's arm in an effort to get her moving but she seemed lost and disoriented. Evan looked back at the aliens coming forward with the circle of humans protecting them.

" Sara, we have to move now!" screamed Evan.

Leah grabbed her other arm and they pulled her down the street stumbling over debris and detritus. They came around the corner of a building into the side street. They waited there against the wall of the building, praying that the aliens would pass by and leave them unmolested. Sara tried to speak and Leah put her hand over Sara's mouth to stop her. They watched in silence. The group of humans with their alien controllers passed them by slowly.

" They're passing by." said Leah.

Several more moments passed in silence, then Sara slumped down to the sidewalk and lost consciousness. Evan wiped blood away from the side of Sara's face and checked her injuries.

" They're gone." said Leah.

" She hit her head pretty hard." said Evan.

John picked a knapsack off of the street and used it

to prop up Sara's head.

" She may have a concussion." said John.

" That crowd of people they control is getting bigger." said Leah.

" Yea. And they recruit more of them at will." said John. " I'm not sure how that process works but I think . . . "

" Wait." said Evan.

There was immediate silence. Evan stood up and looked back down the street. Not twenty feet away stood an alien looking at them. It tilted its head to one side as if curious, not moving or threatening them. The metal rod raised from the backpack on its back and sprayed a short burst of the water like liquid. The alien seemed not to notice the action of the backpack at all and never took its eyes off of them.

" Oh no." said Evan.

Suddenly, Evan's body tightened and became stiff. His face spasmed and his eyes became wide. Leah reached for her pistol only to remember that she had lost it previously.

" Fight it Evan. Stay human. Fight it." yelled John.

John looked over at the alien who seemed to be consumed in concentration. It stared at Evan and didn't move. Leah picked up a rock and hurled it at the alien. The alien lost concentration for only a moment and the rock was deflected and fell harmlessly to the ground.

" Fight it Evan." said John.

Sara lay on the ground and blinked her eyes. She felt dazed by her fall but her head cleared quickly. She saw the alien in the street ahead of them and saw that it was taking possession of Evan. She looked around for something she could do. The business they were next to was a beauty salon. She came to her feet and stumbled inside the door. She returned a moment later with a hand held mirror in her hands. She held the mirror between Evan and the Alien as if to reflect whatever force the alien was using. It worked. Evan's face returned slowly to normal and his breathing slowed.

The alien looked with curiosity at the new event that had taken place. It was stalled, but only for a moment. A storm force began around the group of humans. It increased around them as debris was picked up by the unknown force from the alien. John picked up a bottle from the street and threw it at the alien. The bottle traveled half the distance between them but then stopped in mid air. It ricocheted back and struck the mirror in Sara's hand, cracking it badly. The alien laughed. A high pitched chuckle that echoed out of the mouth between the open mandibles. Its head tilted back with laughter. Leah grabbed Evan by the arm and pulled him into the beauty salon. John and Sara followed closely, with Sara still holding the mirror up between herself and the alien. They hid behind chairs and counters in the beauty salon and waited for what might happen next. The alien walked up to the glass of the store front and peered inside. Then it turned suddenly in the direction of the street, as if listening to some voice only it could hear, then it simply walked away. The four sat on the floor of the salon catching their breath.

" How did you know the mirror would deflect its power?" asked John.

" I didn't. It was just a guess." said Sara.

" A good guess." said Leah.

" The power station." said Evan, suddenly.

" What?" asked John.

" The power station. That device has been sucking power from the grid like a sponge. And humans don't have that kind of mental power that we're seeing. They must be getting it from the aliens. They must be able to funnel power through themselves and into a human host. They doubtless have mental ability of their own but I'm guessing it's not enough to supply a human army with the same power." said Evan.

" You mean they're converting electrical power into something they can use with their minds. Something they can funnel to others." said Sara.

" That's what I think. They're a completely alien species. Who says that their technology has to be based on manipulating the physical world. Maybe they've gone a different route. Maybe their technology is based on manipulating psychic potential." said Evan.

" What about the power station?" asked Leah.

" If they're pulling energy from the power grid and funneling it to their human slaves, then maybe if we cut the power it will cut off their control to the humans." said Evan.

" Could it be that simple?" asked John.

" No way to know, but we have to try something." said Evan.

" Where's the power station?" asked Sara.

" There's a substation about ten blocks from here. We can probably cut the main circuits from there." said Leah.

" Okay. But we'll need weapons as well. They may have the substation protected." said John.

" The Gun Emporium. Two blocks down on Main." said Leah.

" We have a plan." said John.

Run

The group ran down the side street in the direction of the Gun Emporium with Leah in the lead. They crossed Third Street and saw that a similar path of destruction had already passed ahead of them. They checked the road carefully but saw no sign of aliens or the humans controlled by them. They paused to catch their breath while Evan checked the wound on Sara's head. There was only a small trickle of blood that remained. Sara looked around distantly. Their small town seemed to have been destroyed so quickly.

" How many do you think there are?" asked Sara.

" No telling at this point. They could have brought thousands through the portal by now. They could be covering the entire city by now." said Evan.

" Keep moving." said John.

They crossed to the Gun Emporium, quickly opened the door and darted inside. They turned to survey the street through the storefront to see if they had been seen, but nothing was moving on the street. Suddenly, they heard the rustling sound of movement behind them. Leah turned slowly, wishing that she still had her service pistol. She saw several rifle barrels raised in the air and realized that they were not the only ones who thought to come to a gun store. There were several people hiding behind the counters and display cases in the store.

" Who are you?" said a man behind the display case.

" We just came from the Police Station." said Evan.

" What's going on out there?" asked another man from the corner of the room.

" Pretty much what you see out the window." said Evan.

" Have the military got here?" asked a woman.

" We don't even know if they know about it yet. All communication lines are down." said Leah.

" What are the police doing?" asked the display case man.

" There's not much they can do at this point. They're separated and disorganized because they can't communicate." said John.

" She's a police officer." said the corner man.

" She's with us now. There's nothing she can do." said Evan.

" We just have a small local station here. We sent some officers, but none of them came back." said Leah.

" Did you see them?" asked the woman.

" Yes. We saw them." said Sara.

" They're aliens aren't they?" asked the corner man.

" Yes they are." said Sara.

" How did they get here? I didn't see any news stories about flying saucers or anything." said the display case man.

" They're very smart aliens. They didn't need one to get here. They're technology has been here the whole time." said John.

" We're going to the power station to shut it down. We think that might stop the control they have over humans." said Evan.

Evan reached forward and grabbed a shotgun off of a wall display. Then he started shuffling through boxes for shells.

" It won't work. We tried to shoot them. But the bullets won't go through. They have some kind of shield or something." said the corner man.

" Yes. But it will stop a human that they have controlled." said John.

John grabbed a rifle and a box of shells. Sara found a pistol and began looking for ammunition. Leah rummaged through the store until she found a 45 revolver, then grabbed a box of shells and started loading it.

" You can come with us if you like." said Evan.

" No thanks. We're waiting here until dark and then we're heading out. Going to hide in the forest until the military shows up." said the display case man.

" That's not a bad plan." said Sara to Evan.

" Good luck." said Evan.

" You too." said the corner man.

Evan headed for the door followed by the others. He stopped before leaving.

" Are you the owner of the store? Can we pay for these later?" asked Evan.

" The owner of the store's outside lying in the street. You can pay him if you like." said the display case man.

Evan took a moment to fully understand the comment and then exited the building.

" Don't worry, we're going to stop them." said Evan, to no one in particular.

Substation

The electrical substation was a large concrete commercial building with a tinted glass storefront that sat on a small bluff at the edge of town. Lattice towers carried high tension power lines to the north and south at the rear of the structure. Service vans were lined up on one side of the parking lot while trailer mounted emergency generators lined the other side. Evan and the others approached the substation carefully. They kept themselves hidden as much as possible and for the first time in their lives they looked at the mundane building as something potentially threatening. Evan rounded a parked utility van and stopped short. He pulled back to the cover of the van. He held out his arm to hold the others back.

" There's someone there." said Evan.

John and Leah both looked around the corner of the van and saw five men standing at the bottom of a short flight of steps at the front of the building. Behind them, at the top landing of the entry stair, stood an alien.

" Stay here." said John.

John moved behind the row of service vans to get a closer look. The alien stood at the top of the stairs looking at a collection of items it had spread out on the concrete expanse in front of the door. It held a computer keyboard in its hands and looked at it. It tilted its head to either side as if trying to figure out its purpose. It shook the keyboard and looked at it again. Then it took the keyboard and hit it several times against the horns on its head. Then it looked at the keyboard again. John slipped back around the van to his friends.

" We've got to take out the alien first. I don't think the humans will stop us after that." said John.

" How?" asked Evan.

" Maybe we could take a shot at it from around the van." said John.

" Get me within fifty feet of it and I'll put one of these between its eyes." said Leah, holding her 45 revolver.

" What if we miss? Or what if the alien stops the bullet?" said Evan.

" We need a diversion." said Sara.

" What?" asked John.

" A diversion. One of us steps out in front of the building and draws their attention. We make the alien focus on that person. Then the others can take it out while it's busy." said Sara.

" That's a good idea." said Evan.

" Yea, as long as you're not the one standing out there trying to get the alien's attention." said John.

" Show some nerve." said Leah.

John looked at her sharply.

" Okay. So how do we do it?" asked John.

" I'll do it." said Sara. " All of you have got to be better shots than I am. I've never even held a gun before today. As long as you do what you're supposed to do I'll be fine."

" Bad idea." said Evan.

" A minute ago it was a good idea!" said John.

" I'll walk out in front of the van and draw their attention. You three sneak around the side and shoot it." said Sara.

" Wait a minute. There are five humans out there as well. Each with that same ability. What if they attack her?" said Leah.

" We'll have to cover them as well. John and I can fire at the humans from this side. Leah, you circle around and come in behind the vans. You can get a good shot at the alien from there." said Evan.

" What if we miss?" said John.

" Don't miss. Sara, give us five minutes to get into position and then start." said Evan.

Evan, John, and Leah moved off slowly around the van and disappeared from sight. Sara waited, fidgeting and impatient. Finally, she gathered her courage and stepped out from the van. She moved out into the open and began waving her arms.

" Hey! Over here." yelled Sara.

The alien looked toward Sara and the controlled humans shifted their gaze in synchronous movement. The wind began to build around her, bringing the storm that would become a maelstrom. The alien looked at her carefully. It tilted its head and looked cautiously to either side. Then it stepped forward and came down the short flight of steps to stand amongst the humans. The storm stopped and the debris that it picked up fell back to the ground.

" Oh no." said Sara.

Sara felt a vice take hold of her mind. She stiffened and her body went rigid. She felt herself falling away, losing control. Suddenly, she heard a rapid succession of sharp sounds and her mind was free. She was in control again. She looked at the ramp where the alien had stood and saw the alien laying on the ground. Its mouth was open and it seemed to be trying to say something, or only gulping air. A bullet hole in its head oozed a thick yellowish liquid. A moment later it stopped moving altogether.

Evan and John came running out from their hiding places beside the service vans. Leah came forward more slowly, still holding her gun before her with both hands as she studied the five humans who had stood guard before the alien. They had all fallen to the ground. Leah watched them carefully, but they seemed almost catatonic. Several of them rolled on the ground in apparent agony, holding their heads as if suffering from the pain of migraine.

" I should have shot quicker. But the darn thing was moving the whole time. I had to wait until I had a clear shot." said Leah.

" Thank you." said Sara.

" What about them?" said Leah, motioning to the humans on the ground.

" With a little luck they'll be fine. But right now I think we should get going." said John.

The four climbed the stairs and entered the lobby of the substation.

" Anyone know what we should do here?" asked Sara.

" Find the switch room." said Leah.

A quick search of the building revealed a room full of computer workstations, power gauges, and heavy duty electrical gear. The switch room. The group immediately began to survey the controls and switch gear.

" Everything is still working here." said Sara.

Sara hit the space key on a keyboard and the computer screen came to life.

" How do we shut it down?" asked Sara.

" We need to find the main switch gear." said Leah.

" Where?" asked Sara.

They looked at control centers with dozens of switches and buttons. Leah surveyed the wall with electrical gear. Finally, she narrowed her search down to a series of large switches and cable terminations.

" Look. These circuits feed everything North of Main street. That should include Hobbs Lane and everything within several miles of it." said Leah.

Evan and John looked at the bus switches.

" Okay. Let's cut the power and see what happens." said Evan.

" It looks like the computers monitor the electrical grid." said Sara.

Sara sat down at the computer and began to tap on the keys of a keyboard.

" I can't get in to change settings without a password." said Sara.

" We should be able to physically break the bus switches and take the system off line." said Leah.

Leah walked to the wall and moved the three primary bus switches to the open position. A large clap sounded with each switch opening.

" This should open the circuits." said Leah.

" It worked. The system is showing an offline

message." said Sara.

" Okay. If we're right then the device can't pull power off the grid and they shouldn't have enough power to continue an invasion. With luck, the humans under their control won't be controlled anymore." said Evan.

" How do we find out if it worked?" asked Sara.

" We head back to the tunnel project. If it worked we'll know about it soon enough. With a little luck we'll see signs of revolt." said Evan.

" What kind of revolt?" asked Leah.

" I'm not sure. Raiding parties that have broken up. Aliens unable to control the humans in their group. Humans revolting against them. I don't know. Best case scenario is the invasion is over. But we have to find out." said Evan.

" We're working completely off of speculation. The aliens may have enough power on their own to retain control of the people they already have." said John.

" Maybe we should wait here. Or find our way out of town and wait for the military to show up." said Sara.

" No. We have to find out what happened. We don't know anything yet. We have to find out if cutting the power worked. This may be the last chance we have to stop them." said Evan.

" What do you mean?" asked Sara.

" It's our technology. Everything we have is based on our power systems. When they fail we're helpless. We haven't even been able to talk to anyone about what's happening here. Communication has broken down completely. And these things are just getting started. What happens when they get a real foothold here? What if they expand their ability to pull power off our grid?" said John.

" We'd just bomb them." said Sara.

" Something tells me they're smart enough to anticipate that. They may have some defenses we don't know about. In any case, we don't know what's been happening at the tunnel site since we left." said Evan.

" So we go back in. We go as far as we can safely, and with a little luck we find that the power loss has disabled them. But in any case we find out what's happening. We take them out before they establish themselves." said Leah.

" I agree. We have to find out what's going on at the tunnel site. If for no other reason so we can report it to the military when they do show up." said John.

Night Walk

The four walked silently down the dark street of a dim city. They experienced the life of their ancestors from long ago; a night lit only by the faint moon above. Unconsciously, they walked in single file through the debris and bodies that lay littered around them. Occasionally, they saw someone running into a building ahead of them, or peeking out from the broken out window of a building. Hiding, scurrying like rats through the aftermath. Evan led the group, followed by Leah and Sara, and finally John taking up the rear. They trudged along like the survivors of war, suddenly filled with the dread and the sadness of destruction.

" We're going to have to stop soon. I'm exhausted and I need to eat something." said Sara.

" She's right. We'll have to put up for the night somewhere." said John.

" Okay. We're only a couple of blocks from the tunnel project. Let's see if we can get a peek at it. Then we'll find a place to rest until morning." said Evan.

" No sign of the raiding parties. But then no sign of

a revolt either." said John.

They continued to walk through the night. Finally, they turned the corner that led onto Hobbs Lane.

" Stay back." said John.

The group stopped, listening silently to the noises of the Street.

" Leah, you come with me. Sara, you and John stay here and wait for us." said Evan.

Sara looked for a long moment at Evan before they split up, wondering if she would ever see him again.

" He'll be alright." said John. " Let's find a place where we can camp for the night."

Evan and Leah hugged the sides of the building as they made their way slowly and quietly up the street. Finally, they could see the construction yard around a street corner. The area that was once a flat yard had swelled. Now it was a small hill, with the field office in ruins at its base. In the center of the hill, where the tunnel opening should have been, was a large gray structure extending out of the ground. The structure was in the shape of the head of one of the aliens, extending a hundred feet into the air. The horns were arced into the sky, completing the visage of a boundless nemesis. The two stared in shock at the transformation that had occurred in only a day.

" My God. What's happened here? How could they build something like this so quickly?" said Evan.

Leah was speechless with shock and confusion.

" I don't know what this is about but my guess is that it's a warning. They want anyone seeing this to stay away." said Evan.

" Yeah." said Leah, still staring at the structure with disbelief.

" Let's get out of here." said Evan.

Sport Center

Evan and Leah backtracked their way up the street. They saw no human nor alien on Hobbs Lane. The sky was darkening, and exhaustion ebbed at their minds and their bodies. They met up with Sara and John where they had left them. Sara sat on the concrete walkway leaning against the building. John sat next to her. Both looked up with relief at the sight of their friends.

" We broke into a sporting goods store, next door down. We can stay there tonight." said Sara.

" What did you see?" asked John.

" Lets get inside. We can talk about it then." said Evan.

The group went inside the sporting goods store where Leah spread out several sleeping blankets on the floor behind the sales counter, keeping others rolled up to use as pillows. John adjusted a small gas lantern they had found and sorted through bags of chips, cookies, and candy bars they found in the employee break room. Evan passed out water bottles from a small refrigerator next to the check out register.

" Where's Sara?" asked Leah.

" Last time I saw her she was breaking up a mirror in the bathroom." said Evan.

Leah gave Evan a questioning look but said nothing.

" Any ideas?" asked John.

" I'm not sure what's happening. We might be too late. They have somehow managed to construct a huge monument on the site in less than a day. I can't even imagine what technology they could have that would allow them to do that. In any case, I don't think we should attempt to go back in." said Evan.

Evan lowered himself to a sleeping blanket, finally letting his body come to rest.

" He's right. Whatever they're doing, they're here to stay. It looks like a fortress now." said Leah.

" An invasion. And we let them out of the bag." said John.

" What do we do now?" asked Leah.

" Let's talk about it in the morning. Right now I need to get some rest." said Evan.

" Me too." said Leah.

Leah lay down on her sleeping blanket and within moments she was fast asleep. Evan lay down intending to wait until Sara came out of the bathroom. He looked to his

side and saw that John was asleep also. He closed his eyes
for a mere moment, fighting the desire to sleep until he saw
Sara safely next to him, but he lost the battle to his
exhausted mind and body. Without intending it, he drifted
off to sleep.

Never Sleep

Evan stirred on his sleeping blanket and rolled over onto his back. He opened his eyes and it took him several moments to remember where he was. He sat up and looked around. Leah, John, and Sara were still asleep in a circle around their lantern. It was morning now and the light was just beginning to illuminate the interior of the store in which they'd camped. Evan stretched his muscles and sniffed at his underarms, he pulled his head back in disgust. He looked over at Sara and saw four helmets sitting on the floor beside her. He reached forward and picked one up. They were bike helmets with small pieces of broken mirror glued over the entire surface. He turned the helmet around in his hand.

" Good idea. Must have taken her half the night." said Evan to himself.

Evan stretched again and reached toward Sara. He shook her leg.

" Get up Sara." said Evan.

Sara stirred and rolled over. Evan shook her leg again and she rolled over again and finally sat up.

" What time is it?" asked Sara.

" I have no idea. Morning." said Evan.

Leah and John began to stir.

" Nice job on the helmets. You think it will work?" asked Evan.

" I don't want to put it to the test. I think we should put foil over our heads and then wear the helmets over that. I'm not sure if it will work, but it's the best I've got." said Sara.

Sara stretched again and tilted her head back. She opened her eyes and then focused on something in the corner where the ceiling and the wall came together. Her eyes grew wide and then she screamed and pointed up. There in the corner of the ceiling was a small creature looking down at them. Its body was like a small ball of pasty skin with two large eyes staring out at them. Around the ball were eight tentacle-like legs that reached out and gripped at the wall and ceiling. The creature didn't move, but merely stared at them. Evan looked at the creature and then made a wild scramble for his gun. Leah found her gun first and took the first shot. She missed, hitting the wall within several inches of the creature. It moved then, scrambling along the corner of the wall until it was over the door. Then it dropped down the wall and exited at the top of the doorway.

" What was it?" asked Leah.

" It's not from this planet." said Evan.

" I think it's a spy." said John.

" A what?" asked Leah.

" A spy. I think it was sent out by the aliens to look around, Keep an eye on things. Surveillance." said John.

" We should get out of here." said Sara.

" I think she's right. If they're doing reconnaissance then the aliens must know we're here." said Evan.

" Everyone put on a helmet, just in case." said Sara.

Everyone reached forward and took a helmet from the small pile by Sara's sleeping blanket. She ripped off a piece of tin foil for each person and they formed these around their heads, finally ending with the mirror covered bicycle helmet on the top. John grabbed a backpack off of a rack and began to fill it with water bottles and snack foods. Evan looked out of the store front window in both directions. Leah checked her weapon and put it back in its holster. Then the group came together and approached the front door.

" Where should we go?" asked Evan.

" At this point I'd say anywhere but here." said Leah.

" But we have to do something. We've got to have some kind of plan." said Sara.

" We could head for the mountains. Like those people in the gun shop. Wait for the military to show up." said Evan.

" The military are going to need us. We've been there from the start. We have information that might be vital to them." said John.

" Well, we can't give them the information if we're dead. If you think we have information that's vital then we should be leaving here as soon as possible." said Leah.

A moment of silence followed.

" She's right. We've done all that we can do here." said Sara.

" Okay. Plan B. We get out of town, find the military, and tell them what's going on here. And if we get separated, don't stop. Just keep right on going until you reach someone." said John.

Evan checked the view from the store front again and suddenly jumped back. Four aliens were suddenly visible coming down the street. They came around the corner and walked through the front door of the sporting goods store without hesitation. Leah reached for her pistol, but the weapon was ripped from her grasp by the psychic power of the aliens before she could raise it. The aliens took up positions in a circle around them. The humans drew instinctively closer together, huddling away from the aliens and looking around furtively.

" Evan, what are we going to do?" asked Sara, quietly.

" I don't know. They haven't tried to take over anyone yet. Either that or the helmets are working." said Evan.

One of the aliens walked forward and stood just inches from Sara. The probe from its backpack rose up and sprayed the grayish liquid in an umbrella pattern over its head. Sara was hit with the over spray from the device and cringed back as much as she could, coughing and spitting as some of the liquid got into her mouth. The alien looked around her head at the helmet she wore, finally reaching out with its hand and grasping it from the top. The alien screamed and pulled its hand away, now covered with yellow blood. It had cut its hand on a sharp edge of the broken mirror. The look on its face tightened and it brought its arm up in a menacing way as if to strike at Sara. Suddenly, it stopped and turned its head to another of the aliens. Some silent communication took place between them and the alien lowered its arm. Sara grimaced and lowered her head, trying to avoid eye contact with the alien. One of the other aliens laughed for a moment. That high pitched cackle. The alien who confronted Sara seemed to lose interest. It turned its head and then walked to a circular rack of sport jackets. It shuffled through the jackets and then picked one off of the rack. It looked at the jacket with interest but then dropped it to the ground after several moments. The other aliens wander off to different areas of the sporting goods store. One grabbed a bow from a wall display and pulled several times at the string and bow simultaneously. Another seemed to marvel at the intricacies of a tennis racket, while the last alien became fascinated with its own image in a mirror. The humans watched them with bewilderment as the aliens appeared to disregard them completely.

" Should we just leave?" asked Sara. " They don't seem that interested in us."

" They sure seem curious though." said Evan.

" What are they doing?" asked Leah.

" They're checking out the sporting goods. Lets move toward the door slowly." said Evan.

The group moved slowly toward the door as a unit, looking back all the time at the aliens who still seemed fascinated with the contents of the store.

" When we reach the door just make a run for it." said Evan.

They reached the front door of the store and opened it only to find another group of aliens standing outside waiting for them. The humans stopped moving, suddenly immobilized by fear and uncertainty.

" Now what?" asked Sara.

" Just keep very still. Don't provoke them. If anyone

has the opportunity to run. Take it. Run as fast as you can." said Evan.

Sara looked into the street and sensed something there. She saw the outline of something huge standing before them in the street. Some creature, blending with the background like a chameleon. The other aliens came out of the sporting goods store and walked out into the street. One of them turned and stepped up to the humans. Then it pointed out into the street and an animal became visible in the place that Sara had sensed movement. Having discarded its chameleon cover, she saw an animal approximately thirty feet long and fifteen feet wide. Huge and completely flat like the flatbed of a truck. It had four limbs, one on each corner, and three toes at the end of each limb. It had a head of sorts, a wide flat appendage at the front with a wide mouth stretching seven feet across. The creature was a grayish yellow in color and had no eyes that could be discerned. Sara caught her breath at the sight and the other humans took an involuntary step back from the street.

" What is it?" asked Leah.

" I'd say it was their version of a tank." said John.

One of the aliens tapped Evan on the shoulder. Evan was startled and frightened by the contact. He backed away from the alien but turned toward it in the process. The alien motioned toward the tank creature with its hand. Evan looked at it but didn't understand. The alien motioned toward it again but still Evan didn't understand. Then the alien walked up to the creature and made motions as if it was stepping up onto the creature's back.

" I think it wants us to climb onto the tank." said Evan.

" What?" said Sara.

Several of the aliens pushed the humans from behind until they moved forward toward the tank creature. A tongue came out of the creature's mouth and snaked out twenty feet toward the humans. Suddenly, an alien grabbed each of the humans from behind, allowing the tongue to touch each of them briefly on the face before finally withdrawing back into the mouth again.

" That was bloody disgusting." said John.

Evan was pushed forward once again and finally used his hands and feet to climb up the leg of the creature.

" This thing feels like rock." said Evan.

The others climbed onto the tank and the creature began to move. The aliens flanked it on either side and the group progressed down the street, stopping at the front of what was once the tunnel project yard. Gone now was the fence and the field office. In its place was a small raised hill and the monument structure that reached into the sky. Construction machinery and the debris from the field office were pushed off to the side. The entrance to the underground area was a large opening at the base of the gray structure. Around it all stood sixty or seventy humans under the control of various aliens. The aliens on either side of the tank creature seemed to exchange unseen communication with the aliens standing guard at the site. Then the tank creature moved forward again and entered the structure through a thirty foot wide opening at the base.

The tank creature was flanked on either side by the alien invaders. The tunnel ramped downward at a steep angle and wound its way in a labyrinth of twists and turns. The tunnel walls were pale gray in color, with rounded corners and an organic feel to the shape and pattern. As they progressed further down the tunnel they noticed a round snake-like creature in the upper left hand side of the tunnel. It was about 6 inches in diameter and seemed to travel endlessly down the length of the tunnel without a head or a tail. It undulated continuously, and occasionally they could see the side of the snake creature open up as it seemed to belch out air into the tunnel space.

The tunnel opened to a wide cavern with a huge mouth-like opening on the sidewall, complete with lips and mashing teeth. They watched as two aliens threw pieces of organic material into the mouth. It chewed the material in a slow circular pattern. The material they were feeding the structure included bits of wood and vegetative matter, but mixed in with the material could be seen the remains of human bodies that had been killed in the invasion. Sara was shocked by what she saw. The others were in a state of stupefaction, but more anguishing still was the lack of concern their captors appeared to have in regard to showing them this sight. It was as if it were a commonplace event to the aliens, with no need of special consideration or attention. The tank creature merely continued down the tunnel, as if nothing of importance had been seen.

" What's going to happen to us?" asked Sara.

" You saw what they were feeding this thing? I'm not going to end up like that." said Leah.

" I think this whole place is an organism. I think they feed it to make it grow." said John.

" It's very humid in here. Their planet must be a moist wet world." said Evan.

" That's probably why they carry the backpacks with the sprayer. They're probably keeping themselves hydrated that way." said John. " They must come from a very wet planet."

" A water world?" asked Leah.

" The earth is a water world, I'm talking about a world where it may rain continuously." said John.

" But what do they want from us? If they just wanted to feed us to this thing they could have killed us outside." said Leah.

" I don't think they want to kill us." said Evan.

At that moment they saw something ahead in the

tunnel. A green flying creature zipped past in the air above their heads. Sara screamed and ducked as the creature almost collided with her head. The creature was approximately nine inches long and resembled an aphid in shape. Two of the aliens on either side of the tank creature laughed at Sara's fright. In another moment the flying creature was out of sight down the length of the tunnel.

" What was that thing?" blurted Leah, clearly alarmed.

The others were in a state of shock, and no one cared to answer her.

The tank creature finally stopped at another large cavern space. At the rear of the space the humans could see the original portal with its platform. They realized with some surprise that they were looking at the original tunnel project excavation. But now the walls and ceilings were covered with the gray material of the organic building. The cavern was populated by aliens who moved aside to make room for the tank creature. In the center of the space they saw an alien sitting on a raised cushion. It wore an elaborate headdress of metal in the shape of a twisting vine. To the side of the alien general was a device that appeared to be the first non-organic machine the humans had seen. It was a flat circular dish approximately six feet in diameter with legs protruding from the bottom allowing it to stand on edge. It looked like an alien version of a large computer screen, and on its surface could be seen images of alien raiding parties as they moved through the city.

One of the aliens escorting the tank creature gestured to Evan to climb down. Evan stood and then dismounted slowly followed by the others. They stood in the center of the cavern space suddenly alone as the aliens backed away and made space for them to stand before the General. For several moments nothing happened. The humans and the alien general stood regarding each other, but for the alien there was no sense of propriety or decorum. The humans in the room stared demurely, with downcast eyes that avoided direct eye contact with the alien. The general's eyes drilled into the soul without reticence or awareness of the uncomfortable nature of its stare. Like a scientist studying a frog under a microscope.

An alien entered the room carrying a black rectangular box in its hands. The box was approximately two feet long, one foot high, and one foot wide. From the top of it extended a line of clear tubes of varying size along its length. A clear fan-like structure extended from the box in front of the tubes. The alien held the box while another brought out another larger square box. The second alien set the larger box on the floor and the humans realized that the larger box was merely a table. The first alien deposited the rectangular box on its top and then moved away. After a few moments another alien came in holding a small scoop.

It opened a small door at the top of the box and poured in the contents of the scoop. Evan strained to see the contents and thought he saw the bloodied remains of a human brain. The alien general took interest in the rectangular box then, staring at it intently for several moments. The clear tubes and fan on the box's top began to glow and fluctuate with light. Then a mouth opened on the side of the box and it began to chew the contents that had been poured into the top. Then it began to speak.

" Who are you?" asked the alien translator.

For several seconds no one spoke. The humans were shocked by the talking box. Then Sara stepped forward.

" We're from the University." said Sara.

The tubes on the top of the box glowed again and several moments passed.

" What is University?" asked the translator.

Sara considered for a moment.

" It's a place of learning." said Sara.

" Are you leaders?" asked the translator.

" No. We're not leaders. But we could take them a message." said Sara.

Another long pause.

" We have no message to give." said the translator.

" What do you want here?" asked Sara.

" We want your planet. Did you not see our forces moving through your streets?" said the translator.

" But can't we live in peace? Why do you have to take over our planet? Why do you have to kill people? We could live together. Share the earth." said Sara.

" There will be no sharing of this planet. We must change your planet to live here. Your planet is dry. Our planet is wet. Continual wet. Rain always." said the Translator.

" But there must be things we could learn from each other. Your technology is different from ours. We could teach you things about our technology and you could teach us things about yours." said Sara.

" We do not desire to learn from you." said the translator.

" Then what do you want? Why have you brought us here?" asked Sara.

" We need your power." said the translator.

" Our power?" asked Evan.

" We need your power. You turned off your power system. You can turn it on again. Our power systems are not yet developed on this planet. This limits us." said the translator.

" What makes you think we'd help you turn the power back on?" asked Evan.

" If you do not help us we will kill you." said the translator.

" We're not going to help you. We'll never help

you!" said Sara.

The alien general stepped forward menacingly toward Sara. Its head bent toward her slightly as if he had just struck her. Though nothing physically touched her, she bent over in pain and stumbled to the ground.

" Help me!" screamed Sara.

" Leave her alone." screamed Evan.

Leah lunged forward toward the alien general. She swung her arm in a wide arc toward the aliens head but her arm was blocked in mid motion by the aliens arm. Leah looked dumbfounded for a moment and then the alien general struck her with its other arm. Her head was decapitated and flew across the room. Her body fell to the floor to the general laughter of the other aliens in the room. Two aliens moved forward and removed the body, presumably to be fed to the growing structure, ever in need of food. Evan knelt down to where Sara sat on the floor and put both his arms around her. The alien general looked menacingly at them.

" You will re-establish the power." said the alien translator.

Evan said nothing. He cringed protectively over Sara, expecting a blow to fall at any moment.

" I'll do it." said John.

The alien general shifted its gaze to John.

" I'll do it." said John.

" Do this and we will let you and your friends go free." said the translator.

" I'll need to leave this place. And I'll need transportation." said John.

" You will have transportation." said the translator.

One of the aliens grabbed John's arm and pulled him toward the tank creature. John climbed onto the creature's back followed by two aliens. The creature moved off and disappeared down the tunnel. The alien general shifted his gaze back to Evan and Sara where they sat on the floor.

" You will remain here. If your friend is successful we will set you free. If not, your bodies will be converted to organic energy." said the translator.

Sara raised her head to peer up at the alien general.

" Why are you doing this? Why do you have to come here?" asked Sara.

" Why? Our people grow. We expand to other planets. We spread our population through the stars. There is no why. It has always been this way." said the translator.

" But what about the people you kill? The environment? What about the ecosystem on this planet? Can't you see that you're destroying the natural world. You're destroying the planet that you are trying to inhabit." asked Sara.

" Why should we care about this? Why should we

care about the existing ecosystem?" asked the alien translator.

Sara paused for a moment. Thinking furiously for a way to get through to this alien intelligence.

" The natural ecosystem of this planet has value. Humans have value. You could study the ecosystem. You could learn from it. You could learn from humans." said Sara.

" We are not interested in the existing ecosystem. We will transform it to suit our needs." said the translator.

" Don't you care about anything? Don't you have feelings? Don't you care about anything but yourselves?" asked Sara.

" We are invading this planet. We will transplant the flora and fauna of our world to this world. We will remake this planet to suit our needs. This base is merely an exploratory force, meant to test your technology and strength. We have made our assessment. Your forces are no match for our strength. Our technology is not subject to manipulation by your people. We will win and your people will die." said the translator.

" You can't do this! You can't . . ." yelled Sara.

Evan put his hand over her mouth and pulled her back, holding her from breaking free as he feared that she would attack the aliens regardless of the outcome. The alien general looked at another alien in the group who then approached Evan and Sara. It motioned them back to an area against the wall. Evan used his feet to push himself and Sara along the floor to the side wall, out away from the center of the cavern floor. The alien stood guard over them but essentially ignored them, while other aliens in the room appeared to have forgotten them entirely.

" Why won't they listen, Evan? They're intelligent. I thought that would mean a . . . willingness to see reason." said Sara.

" They are intelligent. Very intelligent. But unfortunately that doesn't seem to equate with reasonableness. We've been anthropomorphizing. All of us scientists. Assuming that an intelligent race would have the same value system, that they would have any value system at all. They're intelligent, but they never really left the food chain. Not in their way of thinking. These are cold and sophisticated monsters." said Evan.

" But they wouldn't even lie about their plans. They just came right out and told me what they were going to do." said Sara.

" I don't think as a species they have embraced lying. I don't think it would even occur to them. Why would it? Lying is fundamentally inefficient. Unfortunately, it probably means that it's telling the truth about the expeditionary force. They may just be testing us." said Evan.

" We need the military. Even with their ability to absorb power from our power systems we'll still beat them. We can bomb them from the air." said Sara.

Evan studied the actions of the alien general and now saw it work intently at the round view screen.

" Look." said Evan.

The alien general was no longer using the round view screen to communicate with the alien exploratory forces. On the screen the general scrolled through images of alien war machinery. Horrifying machines designed to walk and fly. Huge machines of impossible size and dimension. Designed by alien minds with purposes that could only be guessed at by the humans watching them. The general touched the screen, and as he touched it the list at the bottom grew with the addition of a new item.

" My God. What are we going to do?" asked Evan.

Sara heard a flutter of wings and noticed for the first time the cage protruding from the wall next to her. She studied it and saw that the cage was approximately two feet wide and ten feet in length. The bars of the cage were spaced approximately two inches apart and were made of the same material as the cavern walls. Inside the cage were the green aphid-like creatures like the one that had almost hit her as it flew down the tunnel. The cage was full of them. Each approximately nine inches in length with wings that fluttered as they clung to the bars of the cage. One of the creatures was close to her.

" "Help me!" said the aphid creature.

Sara watched as an alien approached the cage and reached through the bars. As if on cue, the bars spread open allowing the alien's arm to enter. The alien considered for a moment and then picked out a plump aphid. It grabbed the animal, pulled it out of the cage and began eating it.

" Oh God!" said Sara. " These creatures are also intelligent, and the aliens are just eating them."

" Help me!" said the aphid creature.

Several hours passed. Evan sat hunched over against the wall while Sara lay asleep in his lap. He had always been confident in the decisions he had made in life, but that had ended now. It had ended on this very day. He sat in a stupor. Nothing came to him. He saw no way out and no way to rescue the situation from the overwhelming aberration that was the alien technology. He considered for a moment what he would do when the aliens set them free, and he had no doubt that they would do as they promised. Run into the mountains he guessed. Try to stay alive as long as possible. Maybe adapt to a new way of life. One spent in the corners and dark crevasses of the world. Like rats scurrying in the night.

Evan sensed something, a stirring amongst the aliens. He looked up not really knowing what to expect and suddenly saw the tank creature enter the room. John Philips and several aliens preceded it. On its back was one of the generator sets they had noticed at the power facility. The tank creature carried it with ease. John looked around the space and finally saw Evan and Sara against the wall. He looked at Evan and nodded his head slowly. There was something in that nod, but Evan didn't yet understand. John was trying to tell him something. The tank creature reached the center of the room and then lowered itself flat against the ground. The alien general stepped forward.

" You have returned." said the alien translator.

" I have brought a generator. A power generator. This will restore the power you need." said John.

Evan became tense. He caught John's gaze and slowly shook his head from side to side. Sara woke up and shifted into a sitting position. John moved up onto the back of the tank creature and opened the side panel of the generator. He made several adjustments and then pushed a button and the generator motor turned over and started. It took a moment to reach full power but then the generator roared. It was as if in a moment the space of the cavern had completely changed. Along the side walls and ceiling of the cavern space tendrils of light began to glow and illuminate the interior. It suddenly seemed like a magical transformation. What was once gray and stony walls were now illuminated with coils of changing color and light. The aliens in the cavern all began to vocalize a high pitched cheer that lasted several seconds and then died down to silence.

" You have completed your task. We will let you and your friends go." said the alien translator.

" I'm not finished yet. I can increase the power

output of this device." said John.

John reached up to the generator and pulled an ax from its bracket on the side panel.

" This device uses a conductive liquid to generate power. I can increase the power output by soaking the floor with this liquid." said John.

John took the ax and hit the fuel tank on the side of the generator. Fuel began to spill out. Then he took a five gallon gas can from the back of the tank creature, opened the lid, and began pouring gasoline onto the floor. Evan and Sara watched in horror. They could see John's plan and what the results would be.

" Give this a few minutes and you'll see the power output increase." said John.

The alien general cocked its head and looked at John as if it suspected something was wrong, but it didn't understand what John was doing or how fossil fuel technology worked. It didn't understand the machinery of the generator, but it knew that something wasn't right. John took a book of matches from his pocket and held it up in his hand. He looked at Evan and Sara and exchanged a final look of understanding. Evan stood up and took Sara's hand. They were poised to run. When it happened, they would have only a few moments.

" What are you doing?" asked the alien translator.

" Watch." said John.

With that word John struck the match and threw it to the floor. The match hit the gas soaked floor and instantly the floor was engulfed in flames. Within seconds it had engulfed the entire cavern space where the portal sat. The aliens in the room seemed powerless to react. They looked at the fire around them, but it was more out of curiosity than fear. On their world of constant rain they had never before seen fire.

Several of the aliens suddenly started to scream a high pitched scream as they scrambled away from the flames. The alien general jumped back away from the flames and watched as several aliens tried to extinguish the fire but were themselves burned in the process. The tank creature rumbled to life in a panic. It turned the generator from its back and trampled aimlessly, killing several of the alien creatures. Sara and Evan ran for the exit, completely forgotten by the aliens. Evan hesitated at the exit from the cavern and looked back. He looked for John but couldn't see him. The flames were high now, and if he was still alive, John was cut off from the exit. The cavern room had become a death cell. Aliens ran everywhere, unable to put out the fire that engulfed them. The alien general jumped to the portal and a large flash of light erupted as it passed through. The remaining aliens in the room followed the general so that Evan saw flashes of light as a backdrop to the growing flames of the fire.

As the organic structure began to feel the flames and the heat, the very floor that they stood on began to shake and rumble. Evan and Sara ran. The tunnels themselves seemed to undulate and move. Aliens ran down the tunnel past them in the opposite direction. Evan looked over his shoulder and could see the aliens running through the flames in an attempt to get to the portal. Sara pulled him forward.

" Come on! We have to get out of here." said Sara.

They ran another thirty feet and the tunnel shifted. Sara was thrown off of her feet.

" Evan!" screamed Sara.

Evan turned and ran back. He grabbed her hand and almost dragged her down the tunnel, finally pulling her to her feet.

The flow of aliens coming back into the tunnel increased. Hundreds of them stormed past Evan and Sara without even noticing their presence. They were trying to exit this world now and return from where they had come, but the heat radiating through the tunnel told another story. There was no escaping the flames.

They ran.

The snake-like creature at the upper part of the tunnel had stopped moving. No more air was belched into the space. Smoke began to obscure their path. Finally, light appeared in the tunnel in front of them. Aliens still passed them, coming into the alien complex while they were trying to leave. They avoided contact and the aliens seemed to have no time to intercede. Evan and Sara exited the tunnel and ran another hundred yards until they could hide behind a car that was parked on Hobbs Lane. They turned. They saw the huge alien structure bend and move. Smoke poured from the tunnel opening and from the mouth of the head shaped structure. The structure itself began to bend downward and a low rumbling sound could be heard all around them. The ground seemed to shake and roll for a moment, then the whole raised area of the tunnel project sank down into collapse. The alien head fell inward on itself. Then there was only smoke and silence from the tunnel project.

Aftermath

Evan and Sara stood together on the street of Hobbs Lane. A military contingent had arrived within an hour of the burnout, though Evan and Sara had barely noticed. Now they merely looked on in silence, empty of feeling and emotion as military crews in protective equipment brought charred alien bodies out of the cavern. Someone had given Sara a blanket and she had drawn close to Evan so they could share it. Standing with their arms around each other. Though it wasn't cold, the blanket seemed a universal therapy to the shock they were experiencing.

The body of the tank creature had been hauled out and now lay at the side of the road on its back. It was blistered and blackened by the fire. A man in military uniform came up to stand beside them. He appeared sympathetic and differential to their mood, standing next to them for several moments before speaking.

" This is where it started?" asked the military officer.

" Yes. It happened here." said Evan.

" The fire stopped them?" asked the military officer.

" Yes. They come from a very wet planet. I don't

think they have ever experienced fire like that before." said Evan.

" We're digging our way down, but it's likely to be days or weeks before we reach the portal you spoke of." said the military officer.

" Yes. You should leave it buried." said Sara.

" And you didn't see what happened to your friend, John Phillips?" asked the military officer.

" No. He either burned in the fire, or . . ." said Evan.

" You realize that you're all heroes. You stopped them before they could get a foothold. Who knows what would have happened if you hadn't put a stop to them." said the military officer.

" Yes. But we also opened the door for them." said Evan.

The Military officer slapped Evan on the shoulder and then walked away. Sara and Evan stood there in their exhaustion looking blankly as the cleanup progressed. For no reason that he could identify, Evan looked back over his shoulder. Standing fifty yards away was Rebecca Curtis, the old woman who had warned them before any of this happened. She only stared at them, but met Evan's gaze when they made eye contact. Nothing was said, but Evan thought he noticed the slightest node of her head before she turned and walked down the street. Evan turned back to watch the progress of the cleanup, thinking that if there was any closure to this incident, it was in that simple nod of the old woman's head.

End